DRIFTING

By the Author

Not Broken

The Willing

Drifting

DRIFTING

by

Lyn Hemphill

2022

DRIFTING

ISBN 13: 978-1-63679-242-2

This Trade Paperback Original Is Published By
Bold Strokes Books, Inc.
P.O. Box 249
Valley Falls, NY 12185

First Edition: November 2022

Credits
Editor: Barbara Ann Wright
Production Design: Susan Ramundo
Cover Design By Tammy Seidick

Dedication

To the Nano Crusaders, especially in MerMay!

CHAPTER ONE

Jet lay underwater, looking at the surface far above. The waves seemed rough today, the sunlight filtering through the water weak and scattered. She could feel the current working against the disturbance from the wind above, water eddying and pulling in different directions, tangling its fingers into her sensory hair. She flared her gills and imagined she could taste the distant shores. Sometimes, Amber swore she could taste the warmth of the Caribbean when the Gulf Stream surged, but Jet, for all the times she'd lay still and tried, had never been able to tell the difference.

She linked her fingers over her belly and tried to force relaxation. Let go of all her tension, let the water support her completely. She used to be able to. East Bank had always been her favourite place as a teen. She and Amber would lie on the sand and watch the slow-motion wars between the starfish or anemones, and then hang in the middle of the ocean, suspended between ground and air, and let the current take them.

Now, she found she couldn't let go. Her stomach muscles were tense under her fingers, her head turning at every click and mackerel grunt and distant ship noise.

It was deeply bloody irritating.

"There you are," Amber called, swimming up to her, her long hair twitching at the ends with agitation. It would be a coppery colour farther up in the water, where the sun was stronger.

Sometimes, they swam right up to the surface, and the reds and oranges of Amber's hair and tail would appear gradually like stars. But down here, all her bright colours washed away, Amber looked hazy. Not real enough to pay attention to.

"Your dad said I'd find you here."

Jet snorted. "My dad *said*. My dad. The one without the lower jaw, that dad?"

Amber didn't react and lay back beside her, staring up through the green. Patterns of light formed across the round curves of her face, the freckled cheeks and plump lips that Jet had always been jealous of. At least Jet had a badass black tail, though. Amber's looked like a bloody goldfish on the surface and like sand everywhere else.

"There's more ways than speaking to say something," Amber said, as if Jet didn't *know*, as if she hadn't spent most of their life telling that to the cloaca-brains in their age set. Frustration and anger flared under her skin, and she forced herself to stay still.

Amber glanced over, one tendril of hair reaching out to poke at Jet's cheek. Jet brushed it away too forcefully. Amber raised an eyebrow. "Did you have a fight with him, then?"

"How do you think that would've gone, huh? I'm not a complete bastard, Amber."

"And he's not a delicate flower, *Jet*."

"I know he isn't." She gave up the pretense and jolted upright, crossing her arms to loom over Amber. "He's a warrior so why doesn't he get it?"

"You mean, why doesn't he want to start the war up again? Geez, I don't know, what would possibly make him want to avoid further bloodshed?"

"I am not trying to start it up again. I'm trying to stop it from ever happening again, obviously." Jet waved her arms around, getting her bracers caught in her sensory hair and wincing.

Amber reached over to untangle the strands, and Jet tried to suppress the tickle as Amber's fingers tugged the locks out from between the plates. "It's been nearly thirty years since the war ended," Amber said, not looking at her. "You can't possibly remember it."

"But you do, don't you," she said, jumping on the opening. "You remember things from when you were tiny. You have to remember the war."

"Yeah, bits." She shrugged and released Jet's bracer, now free of hair. "Nothing the elders haven't told all of us. I don't even know how much of my memory is real and how much is made up from their stories."

Jet nodded. "Sometimes, I feel like I remember it. I can't possibly, but…"

"Yeah. Which is why I don't know why you want to go back to that."

"I don't want to go back to that," Jet snapped. "How can you think that? I want to avoid it, keep the little kids safe from it. What better way than to make sure it never has a chance to start?"

"Preemptive strikes?"

"Exactly," she said, snapping her fingers.

Amber raised an eyebrow and *looked* at her.

"I don't mean, like, going into their communities and ambushing them, obviously. I'm not a monster. But this is the third time this month that we've had reports of Knarr passing the boundary lines."

Amber held up her fingers to count on them. "Once, it was a little kid gathering razor shells. Once, it was a group on a hunt who didn't notice they'd gone past the boundary marker, and once, it was just two mer talking. The sentry said they didn't even realise they'd strayed close to the line until she went to talk to them."

Jet snorted. "A likely story."

Amber rolled her eyes. "Sure, I bet the razor-shell kid was a spy in disguise. Not everyone from the North is itching to start up the war again, you know."

"Well, then, why can't they respect the boundaries? The peace treaties are there for a reason. It's not like we're drifting into their space every few days. Why can't they hunt razor shells on their side of the buffer zone?"

"They *were*, Jet. It was an accident."

Jet growled in frustration and flipped her tail, looping over and away.

"Where are you going?" Amber called behind her.

"On patrol."

Amber groaned like a teenager, and Jet heard her tail swish before she caught up. "It's not your shift."

"I'm the chief's daughter, I should do more shifts anyway."

"You're full of shit, Jet."

"What?" She tried to keep the whine of hurt out of her voice.

"*I'm the chief's daughter, I have* so *much responsibility,*" Amber said, pressing her hand to her forehead dramatically. "It's not like chiefdom's even hereditary, idiot."

"I can't help it if I take my family's position seriously."

"You can help it. You're literally the only one who can help it. It being your brain and feelings and all."

"I hate you."

"You love me."

"I put up with you because we're cousins."

Amber shrugged. "Well, then, I'm your favourite cousin." She dived deeper, turning on her back to stick her tongue out. "C'mon, race you to the old wreck."

"Amber, we are *patrolling*."

"You're patrolling. Unnecessarily. Come on, what's wrong, think I'll beat you like the last time?"

Jet held her gaze, keeping her expression blank. Then she put on a burst of speed and shot past Amber, arms flat to her sides and sensory hair tightening around her head and out of the way.

"Cheater," Amber yelled from behind her, and she grinned, water pulling at her lips until she forced them shut again.

The wreck loomed ahead through the haze, the visibility still not too badly affected by the winds up on the surface. Jet could hear Amber powering up behind her, flared her gills, and kicked her tail until the muscles burned. The wreck rose with the rhythmic currents and thumped back down onto the mud below, and Jet narrowed her eyes to judge her timing, shot out a hand and grabbed a crumbling railing.

"Loser," she yelled as her momentum sent her tail flipping over her head.

Amber made a rude gesture at her and let herself slow down naturally, hovering above the upper deck of the ship. Her gills flared rapidly, as fast as Jet's own breathing. "No shame in losing to a cheater."

"You sure about that?"

Amber didn't deign to answer and swam a lazy spiral up a radio mast. The railing tugged on Jet's arm with a downdraft, and she let go, swimming up and out of the way. The ship was breaking into pieces, she noticed, a crack that had been the width of her palm now big enough to swim through, the whole ship starting to flex and groan with every shift in the water. It wouldn't be long before it cracked right down the hull. Jet would have to assess its safety again, see if it was still suitable for the younger teens. Kids were going to play in it whatever they did. At least they could make it so it was somewhat safe.

"Huh," said Amber. She was looking out toward the buffer zone, her hair spread out around her head like a human satellite dish.

"What is it?" Jet swam up the mast toward her, her own hair spreading wide on alert.

"Don't know," Amber said. She closed her eyes and started breathing in that very measured way mages had, her head loose and rocking with every inhale.

"Do a searching spell," Jet said.

Amber opened one eye. "What do you think I'm doing?"

"Well, go on, stop talking to me."

Amber snorted bubbles out her nostrils, the valves that held them shut underwater clicking with irritation, but she closed both eyes again and began the breathing exercises. Jet shifted impatiently beside her, straining her eyes and sensory hair as if she could part the curtains of haze.

Amber started to chant, low and slow, matching the rhythm of her heartbeat. Jet knew from experience that if she was interrupted now, she'd have to start all over again. It didn't make the waiting any easier.

At last, a glow appeared in Amber's cupped hands and consolidated into a roving arrow. It circled once, twice, then settled to point in one direction, out into the buffer zone.

Before Amber could say anything, Jet sped in the direction of the arrow, her tail snapping out behind her. "Get lower, idiot," Amber said breathlessly from behind her. At least she was following. At least she got the severity of the situation. Jet slowed just enough to let Amber catch up, her hands still held out in a cup to keep the searching spell going.

The two of them swam low to the seafloor, high enough that their tails wouldn't disturb the sand and leave a trail. It was probably one of their own. After all, as Amber had said, this wasn't their patrol hour.

Jet wished she could be naive enough to believe that.

A steep bank rose above them, and Amber motioned to Jet to slow as they swam to the plateau, tucking themselves close to the odd outcrops of coral. She heard them before she saw them, and her blood ran cold, then hot.

"Knarr," she said, her voice strangled.

"It's no-man's land," Amber said under her breath. "They've as much right to be here as we do."

Jet gripped an outcropping to hold herself steady as she rose just far enough to look out at the group on the plateau. She dropped back and turned to Amber. "Look for yourself." She jabbed a finger up. "They've got a settlement there, Amber, they're *living* there. I knew it, I fucking *knew* it. They're moving in, they're…they're mobilising."

Amber took Jet's place, pulling herself up and fanning her tail in a figure eight to hold her steady against the rock. "I mean, it could be…"

"They have stone shelters. Look at it, look properly, and stop lying to yourself for once."

Amber bit her lip. "We should tell Cordelia."

"Mam's not going to believe it if I tell her."

"I'll be the one to tell her, then, c'mon."

Jet lifted herself up for one last look, gaze darting quickly around the scene. If these were elders and children, that was one thing. They shouldn't have been there, but Mam would find a way to move them back into their territory and maintain the treaties. But these were all people Jet's age or older, battle-hardened and armed, and her heart was beating so hard, she swore they would be able to hear.

She slipped back down as quietly as she could and nodded to Amber. "Let's go, quick."

Someone shouted, and adrenaline dumped into Jet's blood like a hurricane. She had the spear off her back and on guard in less than a breath.

"Who are you?" Three Knarr mermen swam in front of them, knives out, their black-and-white patched tails rigid and vibrating as they held their position.

Amber swam forward, her hands out. "It's okay, everyone calm down," she said. "Hi. I'm Amber Solan, and this is my cousin, Jet Garrow."

"Garrow," said one of the men with a snarl. "Like the Farn Deeps chief?"

"That's my mam," Jet said, her jaw clenched.

"Let's put our weapons down now," Amber said, shooting Jet a glare. "Let's not escalate this, shall we?"

"You're the ones sneaking up on us," the middle mer said. He spoke with a strong Knarr accent, his words slipping together like eels.

"Sneaking up…you're not supposed to be here. This is the buffer zone for a reason."

"What are you going to do?" he asked.

"What I have to," she hedged.

"Brede," said the one on the left, the slightest tremor in his voice.

"It's fine, Haj," said the middle one, but his fingers clenched tighter around the handles of his long knives.

"We can't let them—"

The third, the one who hadn't yet spoken, twitched forward. Amber gasped, her hand tensing and a little uncontrolled mage-spark forming around her fingertips.

"Witch," cried Haj, and he slashed at her.

The energy and fear that had lived under Jet's skin for so long bubbled up and out, and with a roar, she dragged Amber behind her, knocking the Knarr's knife aside with her bracer. The world narrowed to the three enemies and Amber at her back, the shouting and ringing of metal on metal. Jet's mind went silent, all her attention bent to the movement of the three mermen and of the others now coming down the rise, of the dodging, the lunges, the strikes. The cries of the middle one, Brede, as she cut a long gash up his arm with her spear, the crunch of joints as she twisted an arm away. Haj's wide-open eyes as he swung for her, her own shout as one wild flail cut her shoulder, too close, too close, she had to be *better*.

There were five now in the battle, and more coming down the rise. Behind her, Amber was murmuring, but Jet didn't have time to listen and answer. She had to fight, had to keep them all safe, and she couldn't do that if she let the Knarr overwhelm her. She gritted her teeth against the pain in her arm and switched her spear to her southpaw side, jabbing, slashing, catching the blade deep in the tail flesh of one of the newcomers, who wailed.

The blood in the water was making her sick, getting into her gills and burning her from inside out. An older Knarr was screaming as he rushed down, pulling the wounded away. *Good, keep them busy, keep their hands away from weapons.* A sharp fin caught on her cheek, and her head snapped to the side with the force of the tail beat. She blocked, she lunged. She dodged, she circled Amber to keep her safe.

"Jet," Amber cried, and Jet turned, terrified to see her cousin captured or hurt or worse, but she was hunched over a glowing ball of magic. Jet allowed herself a smile. They were saved. Amber was powerful enough to level this whole settlement.

Amber held her gaze, and something passed between them, something that made Jet want to resist. Then, Amber threw the spell at her.

Jet took one deep breath, but before she could shout, the ocean around her cold-boiled. She'd been caught in surf once before, out near the shore, and the waves had rolled her over and over. It felt like that again, disorienting, jolting. Her body screamed in pain; her tail felt like it was burning.

Then, it was gone. The storm around her disappeared, and she fell, impossibly heavy, and she hit the ground.

She pushed herself up on shaking hands, her muscles protesting the movement. She gasped air, vomited blood and water, gasped air again. Air. Shit.

She sat up and pushed her wet hair back with shaking, sand-covered hands. A cold wind blew goose bumps over her arms, more badly cut than she'd thought. And her tail…her tail was gone. She touched legs, split and jointed and curled under her body at a freakish angle.

Amber had made her human.

❖

It took a long time to remember how to walk. She was relieved it was late, the moon casting a weak light through the clouds down over the beach. She hoped Amber had thrown her out at her tribe's usual landing point so she'd be able to find her way home easily.

She allowed herself a moment to lie on the sand and catch her breath. The night air was cold on a soft human body, the fat layers not nearly insulating enough even under her tunic and armour, but Jet was a warrior. She could handle a bit of autumn night cold.

She looked at her hands, at bruises blooming over her knuckles and the blood trickling sluggishly from all the cuts. None of them were of much concern. Nothing old Marra couldn't fix when Jet got back. After she'd made sure Amber was safe.

She felt a blaze of anger. It had to be anger; she couldn't allow it to be anything else. Amber had sent her away, forced her to leave Amber behind with all those bastard Knarr, to leave her in danger like she *knew* Jet would hate.

She pushed to her feet and wobbled a moment before she got control of the muscles again. It must have been years since she was last on land. She'd happily let it be longer. She staggered back into the water, pushing her unwieldy legs through the waves as the beach sloped, taking her deeper.

Surely, she should have turned back into a mermaid by now? She remembered the last time she'd gone on land with Mam, how they'd waited until dark, then had simply dived in, legs fusing back into a tail instantly. Jet dunked herself, but the sea closed over her head, and her legs remained.

She crawled back out and tried to pretend that her heart was beating hard from the effort, from the exhaustion of the fight, and not from the fear. She found a pile of rocks and scrambled up to dive in, but still, her legs kicked, and her tail remained trapped in the magic.

Jet sat on the beach and wrapped her arms around her knees. She was beginning to shiver in earnest now, and the despair was creeping up on her, trying to get its claws into her mind. She wiped eyes which were warm with tears. She couldn't let herself be dragged down by this. She couldn't afford to lose hope. She had to get home, had to get back to Amber. She had to warn everyone about the Knarr, but here she was, trapped on land like a human.

She wanted to bury herself in the sand and let this fear go past to grab hold of someone else. It took more energy to force herself onto her feet than it had during the whole battle. She imagined herself outside her human body, shaking herself. *Snap out of it. You're no good to them dead.*

She rose at last and started to walk into town. Amber's spell, like the amulets they used more often, was designed to make the change from mer to human subtle, to draw as little attention as possible. As such, her clothes had changed shape to fit her new human body, the tunic lengthening to make what the humans called a dress. The armour seemed to have become shorter so it ended at her waist rather than halfway down her tail, which made sense, as human hips bent to a frankly terrifying angle. Amber being a mage, not a warrior, had probably never bothered to consider armour for legs anyway.

She swallowed and tried to pretend that thinking of Amber didn't make panic rise in her throat like gorge. This was no time to freak out. She had to hope that the Farn Deeps clan still kept the same beach hut, that the spare key to the hut was still in the same hiding place. She would get there, she had to. She would sleep and heal and try again, and she *would* get home.

She had to.

CHAPTER TWO

Tessa. Tessa!"

Tessa looked up from her tablet as Sophie rushed over while obviously trying to look like she wasn't rushing at all. "What is it?"

"Elias isn't here yet. I've been calling him, but he's not picking up." She glanced behind her toward the door, delicate fingers fluttering to tuck a stray strand of hair back into her blond bun. "None of us have a copy of the presentation. What're we going to do? The board is on its way."

Tessa glanced around the conference room, the great wooden table such a change from the rickety things they usually pushed together for meetings in the office. "Where's David?"

"He's talking to Mrs. Pontegrass, but she keeps checking her watch." Her big blue eyes were beginning to shimmer with tears, and Tessa was struck once more with how very young she was, fresh out of university. "What are we gonna do?"

One more flicker of her eyes around the high-ceilinged conference room, rushing over the projector set up at the back, the blinds ready over the high windows, the refreshments in the centre of the polished table. Tessa nodded and unlocked her phone. "We're going to ace this, that's what. Get into Dropbox and bring up the most recent version of the presentation, and skim through, make any quick changes you need to. You know it best of all of us. I'll take over from David and get Mrs. Pontegrass talking about her grandkids. When David comes out, tell him to set the projector up in the conference room. He's the only one who can ever get the bloody thing to work. And while you're doing that, keep calling Elias."

Sophie nodded and took Tessa's phone, scrolling with shaking fingers. "Okay, I can do that. I can do that."

Tessa took her phone and started another call to Elias before tucking it into the crook of Sophie's neck. Sophie held it with her chin and smiled. It made Tessa want to pat her head; the kid was so damn young.

"You can do this," she affirmed, and went to find Mrs. Pontegrass.

"Tessa," Sophie called, and she turned back. "What if Elias doesn't get here on time? What if…"

"Then you'll start the presentation."

"What? I can't."

Tessa walked back to her and took the phone before it fell. She put her hands on Sophie's shoulders and held her gaze firmly. "Did you or did you not stay up late four days in a row to get this finalized?"

"Yes, but—"

"And who did the legwork for that genius idea about the starch-based plastic supplier in Newcastle?"

"Well, me, but—"

"And who phoned Elias on Sunday morning to tell him about a flaw she'd found in the pricing tiers?"

"I did."

Tessa nodded. "Trust me, Soph. Elias would agree, you're the best one to take on this challenge. And look, when he gets here, if he gets here on time, I'll give you a signal. You can introduce him as the project lead who'll be making closing comments and answering questions."

"And if he doesn't? If it gets all the way to the questions and he's not there?"

"Then David and I will come up with you to pick up any slack. You're not alone in this, and you're going to absolutely smash it, you hear me?"

Sophie nodded, her head shaky but her jaw setting, and Tessa smiled, passed the second phone back, and turned. She tossed her hair back as she opened the reception door, plastering her best non-threatening smile on. "Excuse me, Mrs. Pontegrass, could I steal David away from you? Sophie's looking for technical support."

"Of course." Mrs. Pontegrass glanced at her watch, a delicate gold thing. "We should really make a move to start the meeting."

"Let's do that," Tessa said, nodding to David and gesturing in Sophie's direction. He cast her a grateful look and scuttled off, and Tessa took her place at the CEO's side. "Is young Harry going to the football tournament that my nephew keeps on about?"

Mrs. Pontegrass's eyes lit up. "Of course, couldn't keep our lad away from anything football related. I'm sure young Ben's the same."

"I think Ben's happier on a skateboard, no accounting for taste."

"Ooh, I couldn't stand that, the injuries these young people get on the skate park. I do hope his mam makes him wear a helmet."

"Of course." The lift dinged, a subtle, expensive noise. Tessa followed Mrs. Pontegrass across the thick carpet to welcome the three board members, staying a carefully calculated half-step behind. Still no sign of Elias, she noted as she shook hands and introduced herself. It didn't matter. Tessa had faith in her team, and she had to admit that crisis management like this made her heart pump, her neurons fire faster.

Sophie looked like a rabbit in the headlights as Mrs. Pontegrass and Tessa led the rest of the board into the conference room. David, who'd been with Tessa a bit longer and had seen her in action before, looked a little calmer and nodded while he hunched over the phone and the projector. Tessa sent Sophie two thumbs-up, lowered the blinds, settled at the back of the room, and the pitch began.

Tessa was right. Sophie nailed it. Elias arrived about halfway through, flustered and sweating, and Tessa just managed to intercept him at the door and update him, holding him back until Sophie had come to a natural stopping point. She was sure Sophie would have thrown herself out of the limelight the moment she saw Elias, but Tessa held her back with a carefully hidden gesture. By the time Elias took over to make the closing statement and take questions, he'd caught his breath and had gotten a feel for the room.

Tessa felt like her veins were on fire, a drug-like rush of managing people and their skills and making it *work* when it had been about to go to shit.

God, she was a boring person.

She swallowed the sudden spike of shame and clapped for the end of the presentation. Smiled and shook hands, worked the room, met the board, and read between the lines. Read the looks and the word choices and the micro-expressions, judged their chances of winning the contract, of convincing one more company to improve their green credentials and become a little more sustainable. Try to claw back a little bit of progress from systemic pollution and climate change.

Like you're some superhero, not a boring paper pusher.

When the board and their CEO had left and it was just Tessa's team, there was a beat of silence. Then a collective outbreath.

"Holy shit," whisper-screamed Sophie. "I made a presentation to the board of directors of Pontegrass-freaking-Cooper."

"What did I tell you?" Tessa clapped her on the back. Sophie threw her arms around Tessa's neck and hugged her. "Oh, okay there."

"I'm sorry I'm late, everyone," Elias said sheepishly, his tall frame stooped as he brushed back his slightly sweaty blond hair. "I should've left earlier. Thank God for Sophie, huh?"

"Thank God for Tessa," said David, handing her phone over. Sophie nodded vigorously.

"None of that, we're a team."

The door opened, and Andy leaned in. "I hear the dream team did another great job."

"Have they already said something?" Sophie asked, her eyes wide.

"Nothing concrete," said the boss-man, clapping as he approached. Somehow, Andy always managed to look scruffy, his suit a little ill-fitting, his hair flyaway and thinning, but the smile on his round face had never been anything but genuine. "Just full of praise for you lot. I've got a good feeling about this, lads."

"Good enough for a pint after work?" Elias said.

Andy made a so-so gesture with one hand. "I wouldn't say it's proper celebration fodder yet."

Sophie and Elias groaned. Tessa smiled fondly at them; she was relieved. She'd been looking forward to a night off. Takeaway from that Thai place, a brainless show queued up on the telly. A little treat.

But Andy was looking right at her. "You know what is celebration fodder, though?"

The three traitors turned to her with eerily identical smirks. "A birthday girl?"

Tessa felt her jaw drop as she looked at Andy. "You told them?"

"I can't believe *you* didn't tell us," Sophie said. "I'm buying you tequila just for that."

"No," she wailed.

"*Yes.*"

❖

The pub they'd chosen was a weird hipster joint. Tessa wasn't even sure it would have counted as a pub. It had all the requisite components: a sticky bar three-people deep, a mini-stage in front of a dance area, and a pool table with an orderly queue of pound coins marking their owners' turns. However, the decor was all a bit off-kilter. Case in point: Tessa was currently trying to get comfortable in half a bathtub filled with cushions.

"Buckle up, guys and gals." David elbowed his way through the crowd with a tray of bright red shots and beer chasers. He'd somehow had time to get changed into jeans and a faded Black Sabbath T-shirt. Tessa was sure he was even wearing different glasses, a slight variation on black, square-framed lenses.

"Oh God, Aftershocks," Elias groaned. "The noughties are calling. They want their nasty shots back. Are you trying to see what I had for tea?"

"Nothing wrong with a few e-numbers to go with your alcohol poisoning," said Andy, sitting forward and handing the shot glasses around. Tessa looked at hers dubiously. "All got one? Bottoms up."

Tessa had never been able to do shots. Her throat closed up the moment the overwhelming cinnamon flavour hit, and she had to sit there, her mouth on fire, until she could convince her body that swallowing the foul stuff would be much less horrific than the humiliation of spitting it all over Sophie. Even if it meant her throat was burning after that.

"That's awful," David croaked and downed half his beer. "Who's getting the next ones?"

"I will," said Tessa once she'd stopped coughing.

"No, you don't," Andy said. "Birthday girl doesn't buy her own drinks. I'm up." He wobbled slightly as he stood. "Woo, head rush." He chuckled, patting Elias on the shoulder as he passed.

Tessa shuffled forward, the cushions slippery on the enameled metal of the bathtub, the cut edge sharp on the backs of her thighs. She wished she'd been able to change before coming out. Her first sip of beer felt like ice in her mouth after the cinnamon shots, and for a moment, all her attention was bent to the physical sensation of drinking something she didn't much like while surrounded by loud voices, humid air from the crush of bodies, and the slight vibration of bass through the wooden floorboards.

All too soon, her brain came back online along with the anxiety and awkwardness. She took another deep gulp of beer in the hope that she could recapture that absence, that purely physical discomfort. Anything to avoid the mortification of social interaction.

Sophie leaned forward, her dead-straight hair almost falling into the beer on the table. "You got any plans for your birthday weekend, Tess?"

She shook her head vigorously and tried to swallow the massive mouthful of beer while her face was still attached to the glass, and now she had beer on her legs. She wiped the drops off with her thumb and tried to pretend it hadn't happened. "No, nope, no plans."

Sophie looked disappointed, like everyone was twenty-one and still had their uni friends on speed dial and gagging for a night out. Tessa searched frantically for something to make herself sound less pathetic. "Uh, I'm going to see my big sister tomorrow."

"Aw, I hope she spoils you rotten," Sophie said, that big grin back on her face.

Tessa smiled and nodded and bit back a laugh at the idea of Hannah wanting to spoil her rotten. "I should think she'll make lunch," she said. It was probably true. Hannah did take her role as big sister seriously.

Sophie nodded. It was the kind of nod that encouraged something more, so of course, Tessa's mind went completely blank.

She could do this, she told herself firmly. This was what she *did*, what she was good at. She could read people, work out what they wanted to hear, and give that to them all day for her job. Why couldn't she do that now?

The silence stretched a little. David shifted beside Sophie, leaning a little closer and doing the classic "stretch and put your arm on the back of the sofa" move because he'd been making eyes at Sophie since she'd joined. Tessa couldn't exactly talk about that. Elias was tapping his foot to the music and glancing over at the dance floor, but she couldn't turn around and ask him to dance, not when she hadn't come out yet, not in so many words. She didn't want to give him the wrong idea, but she couldn't exactly turn around and say, "Hey, Elias, I know you want to dance, you should go do that," because it would sound like she was being passive-aggressive, and oh God, she was going to hyperventilate.

"Tequila time, boys and girls," Andy called, and Tessa had never been so glad to see tequila in her life.

❖

David and Sophie were kissing in the corner. Elias was dancing, his head thrown back and quite possibly off-time. Tessa wasn't sure because her head was delightfully swimmy, and her eyes weren't seeing straight, so what did she know? It was entirely possible that someone had been passing a joint around at the corner of the beer garden and had offered it to Tessa, and she hadn't done weed in ages, but how could she possibly refuse? Anyway, it was her birthday. She refused to allow even her own brain-voices to judge her.

Tessa and Andy were propping up the bar. Andy was talking to a guy with long dreadlocks that Tessa was pretty sure had been in the news recently, a local hero who taught disadvantaged kids boxing or something like that. They both seemed very engrossed in their conversation, but Tessa thought they might be talking about different things. Boxer guy was a Scouser, and Andy's

Brummie accent got thicker and thicker with each drink, so she was pretty sure they didn't understand each other. She certainly didn't understand what either one was saying.

She wondered if her own accent got thicker with drink. She turned to the person next to her. "Do I sound really Yorkshire right now?"

"What?"

"I said, do I—"

"How do you humans even hear at these places? It's ridiculous. What did you say?"

Tessa blinked and squinted. The woman next to her was a knockout. Well, Tessa was pretty sure she was. Her vision had always been the first to go on a night out, and she really couldn't see straight. But this woman was definitely curvy, and her hair was definitely glossy, and wow, her face. She was *pretty*.

"You're *pretty*."

The woman sighed. "I can't hear anything. Want to go outside and talk?"

Tessa nodded, and they weaved through the crowd, bouncing back and forth like pinballs. The cold air outside was damp and blowing off the sea, and Tessa shook herself as if she'd been doused in cold water. Autumn was well on its way.

"That's better," said the pretty woman. "Sorry. What did you say?"

Tessa frowned. "I can't remember."

The woman laughed, her head tipped back, and leaned on the railing, nearly missing it with her elbows and having to adjust. "You're very drunk."

"Aren't you?"

She hummed thoughtfully. "I might be. Been a while since I drank this much human alcohol."

Tessa giggled and leaned next to her. She was proud of the fact that she didn't slip. Clearly, she was a lot less drunk than Pretty Woman thought. "That's a funny thing to call it. Aren't you human yourself?"

"Nope," she said, popping the P.

"What are you, then?" Tessa asked, nudging her arm. "An alien?"

"No, aliens aren't real. I'm a mermaid, of course."

"No way. I knew mermaids were real. I saw one when I was a kid, and nobody believed me. Even I stopped believing me. Sorry, is that offensive?"

The mermaid shook her head vigorously and then staggered. Tessa caught her to steady her, and even drunk as she was, she noticed the muscles under the unflattering T-shirt. She stepped back, giving her a once-over. Oversized T-shirt and shorts, on a night out in early autumn? Tessa blinked. Somehow, the mermaid made old cutoffs look good. Definitely some mermaid magic there. Or maybe it was the muscles.

"S'not offensive, we're a secret." She winked, and Tessa thought she must have visible stars in her eyes because a pretty mermaid just winked at her. "Saw what you lot did to the unicorns. We didn't want to go the same way. But you shouldn't stop believing in you. You should always believe in you."

Tessa thought she might squirm with embarrassment and delight at being told such lovely things. She shuffled a little nearer to her new mermaid friend. Close up, and with her senses sharpened a little from the chill, Tessa noticed that the mermaid's arms were visibly muscled but covered all over in cuts and bandages. "You're hurt," she cried. "What happened?"

The mermaid slumped, her head hanging between her shoulders. "Got into a battle with some Knarr."

"You poor thing." Tessa put an arm around her, and the mermaid slumped into her shoulder, soaking up the comfort. Tessa patted her hair, her fingers snagging in tangles. "Are you okay?"

The mermaid shook her head. "I don't know how to get back," she said, her voice muffled, but the distress clear. "Amber cast a spell on me, and it spat me out here, *poof*, right on the beach."

"Oh no, you lost your tail like Ariel from the Disney movie?"

"I don't know what that is," she said, pulling back and pouting.

"Did a sea witch put a curse on you? Do you have to marry a prince?" God, she hoped not.

"Ugh, no," she said, her nose crinkled up. "And Amber's not a witch, she's a mage, there's a difference. I think." She stared out at the sea while Tessa stared at her, at the silver light of the moon glancing off her black curls. "I could always get back before. I don't know what to do now. I don't know how to get home."

Tessa felt sympathetic tears prickling at the backs of her eyes and rubbed the mermaid between her shoulder blades. "It's okay, you'll do it."

"I don't even know if Amber got away safe," the mermaid said, wiping her cheeks. She looked up at Tessa like her heart was breaking, and Tessa wanted nothing more than to wrap her close and make everything better. "What if they attack my family?" she said. "What if I never get back and they…they hurt them all?"

Tessa pulled her up and held her firmly by her shoulders. "You *will* get back. You'll do it. I believe in you."

"You do?"

Tessa nodded, and suddenly, the mermaid was wrapping her up in strong arms and pressing her face into Tessa's neck. "You're so kind," she whispered, and Tessa thought she could melt there. "Thank you."

"My pleasure," Tessa said and let her eyes close.

"Tessa?" called Andy from the door of the pub. "There you are, Tess. We're going on to the next place, you coming?"

Tessa turned to see her whole team, Elias holding out Tessa's coat, one arm around a tall, androgynous person. She glanced back to the mermaid, but the pavement was empty. Tessa blinked. She could still feel the mermaid's warmth. She'd been right here, but now…

"C'mon, birthday girl," Sophie called. "We're going to try that new place over the Chinese on Flowergate."

"There's a Chinese on Flowergate?" Tessa said, still glancing around for a sight of black, tangly hair.

"*And* a club above it." She dragged David over to Tessa, linking her other arm in Tessa's while Elias draped the coat over Tessa's shoulders.

"Hello," she said to the androgynous person. They gave her a slow half-smile and tossed their hair back. "What're your pronouns?"

"Come *on*, or we'll miss last orders," Sophie said and dragged her staggering up the hill.

"Bye," Tessa called back. The androgynous person and Elias laughed and waved, so she didn't tell them that she was actually hoping the mermaid would hear.

David and Andy started running up the street, whooping, and someone yelled at them out of a third-floor window. Sophie started singing about fireworks, and Tessa sighed and thought that perhaps the mermaid had left by magic.

That would fit in with this life, said a dark, quiet voice in her mind. A life lived on the edge of magic.

CHAPTER THREE

Tessa woke up with her phone trying to bludgeon her to death via sound waves. "Oh, fuck," she groaned, squinting at the time. "Oh fuck." She stumbled out of bed and into the bathroom to throw up.

The phone was ringing again when she crawled back out, her pajama T-shirt drenched from where she'd shoved her face under the cold-water tap. "Hello?"

"Tessa? Is that you?"

"Yeah, Hannah, morning."

"Morning? Do you have any idea what time it is?"

Tessa winced. "Yeah, I'm sorry I'm late. I'll be right there."

"God, you sound awful." Hannah's voice seemed to fluctuate between fascinated and disgusted. "Are you coming down with something? If you're ill, you get right back in bed and keep your germs to yourself."

"I'm not ill," she said, putting the call on speaker and rummaging for underwear in her drawers. "I went out last night, drank a bit too much, that's all."

"Are you hungover? Are you late because you're *hungover*?"

Tessa rolled her eyes and bit back a retort. Hannah said it like Tessa had been out all night clubbing seal pups, not clubbing in a shitty little room above a Chinese restaurant. The stupid pun distracted a smile out of her, and she almost missed the peak of Hannah's tirade.

"Are you even safe to drive? I swear to God, Tessa, if I've got to reschedule because you were out partying, I will be so angry. I'd expect that from Joanie, not you."

Sanctimonious bitch, said the raging voice in her head. "I'm fine, Han, I just slept in. I wasn't that drunk."

"Hmm, well, I'm not happy about it, Tessa. I'm going to get you a pack of those breathalysers for your car. I've got some for Joanie, but God forbid she should come visit her sister. You see her, don't you? You can take some for yourself out of her pack. I don't want you driving under the influence, especially not if you're going to have Ben in the car."

"I'm on my way now, gotta go," she said before the angry voice had its way and told Hannah where to shove her breathalysers. She hung up, put her hands on the chest of drawers, and breathed.

What the fuck had she been thinking last night? Hannah was right. This wasn't like her at all. Flashes of the pub and the club tormented her, reminding her of every humiliating thing she'd said, every time she'd misread the situation and not noticed because she was off her face, every time she'd stumbled and looked like an utter twat. And had she talked to some girl about mermaids? Oh, Christ, she'd gotten high too. She'd told some beautiful woman about the time when she was a little kid and thought she'd seen a mermaid out on the rocks.

She looked back at her bed and longed to crawl under the covers, pull them up over her head, and die. Metaphorically or not, she didn't really care right now. But Hannah would be unbearable if Tessa didn't get over to her place ASAP, and she really didn't want to let Ben down.

She grabbed a prepackaged smoothie out of the fridge and threw her sunglasses on, though the sky was grey and unpromising. She fiddled with the smoothie bottle as she pulled out of the parking space but couldn't bring herself to drink it. Her stomach felt both empty and as heavy as lead, and she wanted to pull over and curl up in the back. Not even to sleep, just to hide from the world.

Pull yourself together, she said to her head firmly. *Things aren't that bad, and you've got shit to do.*

And also, *you are never drinking again.*

She pulled up outside Hannah's pretty detached house with its big driveway and wisteria arbour and took a deep breath before steeling herself to get out of her car. The door opened before she'd even knocked. "There you are, at last. Ben! Auntie Tessa's here." Hannah gave her a quick scan, head to toe. "You look terrible."

"Good morning to you too." Tessa followed Hannah inside and pushed her sunglasses on top of her head.

"Who did you go out with?" Hannah was already wearing black heels, her brown hair up in a neat style that probably had a fancy French name and took half an hour to do. She leaned toward the mirror in the hallway and dabbed at her lipstick. A subtle pink, of course. Hannah would never be so uncouth as to wear red, or God forbid, one of those dark shades Joanie used to like so much when she was going through her emo phase.

Tessa caught a glimpse of herself in the mirror, at her short brownish-blond hair, at her long face, her plain jeans and T-shirt. At least Hannah and Joanie had a style. Tessa was just…flat. Nondescript. Nothing.

None of that, now. She took a step to the side so she couldn't see herself and dragged her mind back under control. "Went with some of the guys from work," she said. "We did really well on our presentation to Pontegrass-Cooper, so Andy—"

"Oh God, I should've known it would be something to do with work." Hannah rolled her eyes while somehow still managing to retouch her mascara. "And here I was thinking you'd at least gone out with some friends to celebrate your birthday."

Tessa gritted her teeth and held her snappish response back, as she always did. There was never any point. She'd gone through that phase in her late teens, and it had only made her feel awful and made Hannah look as if she'd been stabbed in the heart.

"Did Joanie at least contact you to say happy birthday yesterday?"

Tessa blinked and fished her phone out to check it. "Yeah, she did actually. Huh. I missed that. It came in last night."

"Oh, for heaven's sake, you two are utterly hopeless. If it wasn't for me hassling you to keep up with each other, you wouldn't even think about your family, would you? I bet you haven't even been to see Dad."

"I have, actually," she said, the retort slipping out before she could catch it. "And I'm going to see him—"

"Ben, hurry *up*, will you? Mummy and Daddy should have left ten minutes ago."

"Next week."

Hannah blinked. "What?"

Tessa looked at her and felt a great swell of exhaustion. "Nothing."

Ben tumbled down the stairs, all gangly pre-teen limbs and bright childish smiles. "Ah, there you are at last," said Hannah. "No, put that skateboard away. You're going crabbing with Auntie Tessa, not to the skate park."

Ben's shoulders slumped, and Tessa took the skateboard from him quickly. "It's fine, Han. I can take him after tea."

"Oh, would you, please, Tess?" Ben turned his adorable dimples on her.

Hannah pursed her lips and glared at Tessa but couldn't seem to find a good reason to argue. Shock, horror. "Fine, I don't have time for this. Off you go, then. Remember, Joanie's due to pick him up at eight, but you know what she's like. If she flakes out on me, I'll come by quarter past. He can have one dessert after dinner, and *please* make sure he brushes his teeth." She raised her eyebrows at Ben, who gave a cheeky smile back. "And he needs at least two portions of vegetables with his dinner—"

"Leave the poor girl alone, Hannah, she's had Ben over before," called Jeremy from the hallway. "Morning, Tessa. Happy birthday for yesterday."

"Thanks, Jez."

"Ugh, don't call him that." Hannah curled her lip. She looked torn between continuing to boss Tessa around and doing what her husband told her like a good little Stepford Wife, then flapped her hands. "I nearly forgot, the breathalysers."

Tessa closed her eyes and prayed for patience. *It's not her fault. It's her way of coping. She's not being awful on purpose.*

When she and Ben were in the car at last, and Hannah and Jeremy were pulling out ahead of them in Jeremy's black Jag, Tessa treated herself to a long moment of just breathing.

"Can I plug my phone in and play Spotify, Aunt Tessa?"

Tessa turned to smile at Ben. "Sure thing. What are you listening to these days?"

"I like Lewis Capaldi, he does loads of great songs. Also, Billie Eilish, have you heard 'Bad Guy'? I'll play it for you."

Tessa let him chatter away and tell her all about his favourite music videos and song lyrics. He was easy to get along with for the most part. Set him talking, make interested noises every now and then, and he was happy. How two such type A personalities as her sister and Jeremy managed to produce such a laid-back child would never compute for her.

She pulled up to her designated parking spot, and Ben hopped out, getting his skateboard from the back seat. "Could we please go to the park now, Tessa, please?"

"Don't mind, kiddo. You can take it with you when we go into town as well, if you like."

He cheered and rushed in front of her. "Helmet," she called, and he nearly fell over trying to run back. "Don't break a bone, please, I'm begging you."

"I won't."

The skate park was barely a block away, a concrete bowl with a grassy park on one side and the ocean over the road on the other. Tessa leaned on the floodlights off to the side, recovering from the dregs of her hangover and clapping every time Ben dropped in successfully. The wind was whipping white crests into the sea, but the sun was struggling through the clouds, bursting through in places and casting spotlights of deep blue here and there in the slate grey. There were even a few hardy optimists swimming in the outdoor pool farther along the park.

Ben came puffing up to her. "Can we get an ice cream?"

She pretended to consider. "Okay, but only after lunch, yeah?"

He fist pumped and bounced around like a little fawn and skated down the pavement until it got too steep. "Tessa, it's raining," he yelled up at her.

"I'd noticed, Ben." The sun had given up for a while, and raindrops were slapping her left cheek like pebbles. She hunched into her hoodie and wished she'd bothered to bring a coat for both of them. "We'll go down to that bandstand by the Battery, okay?"

By the time they had chips and shelter, the rain was coming down in earnest, and they had the space to themselves. Ben snuggled close to her and chattered about school and Pokémon and what he wanted for his birthday. Tessa listened with half an ear and allowed the rest of her mind to drift, lulled by the sound of rain on the sea and the bandstand roof.

"Do you think it'll stop soon?" Ben asked after a rare moment of quiet.

"The weather app says it's going to be like this most of the day, I'm afraid," she said. "It's letting up, though. It's only spitting now." She held up the last of her fish and chips. "You want to save some of your lunch to go crabbing after?"

He shrugged and climbed on the bench and started to balance around the perimeter of the gazebo. "Maybe. Can we go out to the lighthouse first?"

"Don't see why not," she said.

He jumped down, his eyes alight. "Can we go to *both* lighthouses? One after another? Mum always says no, please, *please*, can we?"

Tessa laughed. "Yeah, I guess. I don't have anything better to do."

"Yes!" He rushed out into the drizzle.

"Don't you want to wait till the rain stops completely?"

"No. If we don't go now, it might rain *harder*, and then you'll change your mind."

"Good point, well-made."

He did a little skip and snatched his skateboard up, setting it rolling down the concrete and hopping on, the wheels roaring on the rough surface. Tessa put their rubbish in a bin and followed, shoving strands of hair back out of her face that the wind immediately whipped back in.

Usually, the piers would be packed at this time of day, but it was early September. The summer rush had passed, and the only ones left were locals and the odd child-free tourist that didn't have to worry about summer-holiday dates. And on a day like this, with more clouds scudding in quickly, most people had given up. Ben didn't seem to care, though, and Tessa was relieved that someone was taking charge. Left to her own devices, she probably would have spent the day in bed and then spent the evening beating herself up about wasting a perfectly good Saturday.

She didn't realise she'd stopped to look out over the sea until Ben ran back to her. "Can we go up to the top? It's only a pound for me."

"I assumed you'd want to."

"And I can go up both of them, right?"

"Yes, I promise," she said, laughing.

Ben whooped again, and Tessa hustled him toward the entrance. She wished she could remember being so easy to please.

❖

Ben, of course, insisted on crossing the little bridge and running down the planked part of the pier right out to the green signal buoy, as far out to sea as he could get, before they made their way all the way back to the swing bridge and out to the east pier. By the time they got down from the second lighthouse, though, he was definitely beginning to flag.

Tessa ruffled his hair. "How about we head home and get some dinner?"

"Good idea," he said. He looked out to the last section of the east pier. "I've got to go right up to the red buoy, though, or it wouldn't be right."

"It wouldn't be symmetrical, would it?"

"Exactly," he said. "It'd feel left out."

"Go on, then," she said, rolling her eyes fondly. "Go pet the big red light."

As he ran off, something caught Tessa's eye over on the west pier where they'd started. She frowned and squinted a little; that person looked familiar.

The girl on the other pier leaned right over the railing, looked into the ocean, then moved a little farther up and repeated the action. Tessa frowned and pushed her flyaway hair out of her eyes. She was sure it was the girl from last night, the one who'd rambled about mermaids and sea witches. The one with soft, tangly black hair who'd called her kind and was upset about something. She'd been in cutoffs, but now she was in a long black hippie skirt of some sort and another oversized T-shirt. It might have been the same one.

Tessa's blood ran cold as the woman quickly slung her legs over the railing and without another thought, leaped into the water.

An old couple cried out, words lost to the wind. Tessa rushed to the railing on her own side, her heart a ball of terror at the top of her throat. "Ben, stay there," she yelled and jumped into the water.

The cold howled into her, and she barely got her head above water to gulp in air. She caught a glimpse of black hair and a white face and swam, her arms cutting the water, her legs fierce in their battle against the drag on her jeans, her shoes. She tilted her face to gulp in more air, and a wave washed over her, into her lungs, burning.

Then there was a strong arm around her chest, hauling her up, dragging her through the waves toward the looming wall of the pier, barnacles and rough stone scraping her hands until they reached a steel ladder set into the wall. She grabbed for the rungs, coughing and spitting.

"What the hell were you thinking?" the woman demanded.

Tessa looked up at her furious face. "What was *I* thinking? What were *you* thinking? You jumped in first."

"Yes, and why would you come after me?"

"Tessa," Ben screamed.

"I'm down here," she yelled and struggled to cling to the ladder with numb fingers as the waves buffeted them up and down. The woman seemed to rise and fall with the waves, one hand on the side of the ladder to keep her in place while Tessa felt like she had to use all of her strength not to be thrown around. The old couple leaned over the railing, holding Ben back. A small crowd was gathering, everyone else who'd fancied a drizzly walk out to the piers.

"Do you want me to call an ambulance?" a young man called down, holding up his phone.

"Ambulance?" said the woman.

"Yeah." Tessa thumped her on the shoulder, missing as the waves pulled her away. "In case they had to deal with a half-drowned suicidal idiot."

"Well, you shouldn't have jumped in after me."

"I'm guessing not," the young guy muttered above them, putting his phone away.

Tessa paid him no attention, gasping at the woman. "Oh, fuck you, mate. I was trying to stop you from killing yourself."

"I wasn't trying to kill myself."

"What were you doing, then?" Ben yelled down.

The woman looked very shifty, glancing around the crowd. Tessa narrowed her eyes. "You're not still trying to turn into a mermaid, are you?"

Ben gasped and leaned forward far enough that the old couple grabbed his shoulders to pull him back. "You're a mermaid?"

"No, of course not," the woman said, forcing a laugh and shooting Tessa a poisonous look. "That would be ridiculous."

"Look, could you two please get out of the water before you freeze to death? Or should I get on and call the ambulance?"

Tessa shivered violently, and the woman frowned. "You're cold."

"Of course I am, it's September in the North Sea."

"It's the River Esk, actually," she said thoughtfully.

Tessa rolled her eyes and concentrated on climbing, her jeans, hoodie, and trainers sending a veritable waterfall behind her. She hoped it landed on the idiot's head.

A couple of people helped her over the railing, and the old lady even gave her a towel. "Keep it, love, you'll need it. Are you staying far from here?"

"I live in the town," she said, tugging her hoodie off and wrapping the towel around her shoulders, trying to stop her teeth from chattering. The old man gave his own towel to the not-a-mermaid climbing out behind Tessa. She found herself irrationally angry that the ridiculous skirt didn't seem to be impeding the idiot's legs nearly as much as her own jeans were impeding hers.

"Are you sure you're not a mermaid?" Ben asked. "You swam so fast. I thought Tessa was a good swimmer, but you were over to this side like a shark."

She gave a crooked grin. "Sorry, kid. Mermaids aren't real." She glared at Tessa again.

Tessa rolled her eyes and squeezed the worst of the water out of her hoodie. The small crowd they'd drawn was starting to disperse, and she wanted to get home and warm. Even so, there was something weird about this girl, and she knew she'd only worry about her in the middle of the night if she didn't do something. "What's your name?"

"Jet," she said. "You?"

"I'm Ben," said Ben, who'd clearly found a new hero. Tessa really ought to have been jealous. "This is my Auntie Tessa."

"Do you live around here?" Tessa asked. "You're going to need to get out of those wet clothes as soon as you can."

Jet nodded. "I've got a beach hut down there."

"A beach hut?" She frowned. "Those don't have showers, though."

"No, I suppose not."

Tessa sighed. "Come back to mine, have a shower."

"Why?" Jet gave her a proper side-eye, and Tessa gritted her teeth, offended.

"Because you're wet and cold, and I'll worry about you if you don't. Because I still don't know why you jumped into the sea, and I don't believe that you weren't trying to…" She glanced at Ben, who blinked up. "Trying to do something silly. Good enough?"

"We're going to make tea," Ben said to Jet. "Tessa, can Jet have tea with us?"

"I don't know, will her highness deign to have tea with us? Or is that also too suspicious for words?"

Jet flushed. "Look, I didn't mean to be ungrateful. I would really appreciate a shower, if you don't mind."

Tessa's hackles lowered. "Of course." She cleared her throat, now feeling a little guilty about her own sharp tongue. "You're also welcome to tea."

Jet smiled, and Tessa found herself needing to clear her throat for a whole different reason. She turned stiffly on her heel. "Come on, then, let's get going before I freeze here."

CHAPTER FOUR

Jet found herself gathering the folds of the old skirt she'd found in the beach hut and following the human woman and her nephew toward the human's home. Tessa. Toward Tessa's home; she had to get ahold of herself and stop using the word human as if it didn't apply to her.

That was what had tipped Tessa off the previous night, after all. Jet could kick herself for her weakness. She'd spent a full three days trying to get back to Farn Deeps, trying to get back to the sea, to her own shape and skin, but no luck.

It was terrifying. But that was no excuse to have spent so much money from the beach hut on *alcohol*, of all things. And then to have it make her loose-lipped was unacceptable.

She tuned Ben's chatter out to look at Tessa as they navigated the winding streets of Whitby. She would have to talk to her. Maybe she could convince her that she'd imagined it all? The thought of that left a nasty taste in her mouth, though. To twist someone's perception of the world, that was cruel as well as cowardly. No, she would have to appeal to Tessa's honour.

What did humans think of honour these days? She wished she'd been on more of Mam and Amber's trips to Whitby. She wished she had any idea what she was doing.

They came to a vast building just outside of town, and Jet stared up at it in awe. "Is this your home?"

Tessa looked at her funny. "Yeah, flat three. Well, it's a maisonette, not a flat, but still." She fiddled with the key, her hands shaking and slightly blue in the nail beds. "Come on in. You can take the first shower, it's upstairs, first door on the right. I'll lend you some clothes and make some tea."

Inside, Jet realised that the huge building had been separated into much smaller living spaces, only a few times larger than her beach hut and split further in the way humans had, compartmentalising their homes so the cooking area was separate from the sleeping area. Ben started running up the stairs. "I'll show you how to turn on Tessa's shower," he said.

"Thanks, Ben," Tessa called from inside the kitchen.

Jet followed the child upstairs to find him turning a large white knob and jumping back from the spray of water. "If you want it hotter, you have to move this lever up, and if you want to make it shower harder, you have to turn the knob round that way. Turn it right up so it clicks when you're done, don't go too far past the click, or it'll turn on this lower showerhead, and you'll get a face full of cold water."

"You sound like you're talking from experience," she said.

"Oh, I'm definitely talking from experience."

She laughed, and he ran out of the bathroom, slamming the door behind him. She wondered if he was capable of going anywhere without running. He reminded her of the little ones back home, always moving quickly and tumbling over their own tails.

"Jet," he called, knocking on the door and pushing his way in. She was glad she hadn't started to get undressed yet. "Tessa sent me up with some clothes and a towel."

"Thanks," she said, hanging them on the back of the door as Ben ran off again. She sighed and started to peel out of her wet clothes. They always managed to be much harder to take off on land. She supposed that was why humans tended to wear swimsuits when they went into the water. Of course, Mam and

Amber, and whoever else had come to the human town before them, had never seen the need for a swimsuit. All they had stashed in the back of the beach hut were smelly clothes of odd sizes and shapes, and she had no idea which ones went together, if indeed, humans had rules about that sort of thing. She knew they didn't approve of armour and weapons, at least. She'd tucked hers under the table in the beach hut after she'd gotten some funny looks the first day. If...*when* she worked out how to get her tail back, she'd go get them.

Jet sighed and dropped the wet shirt onto the floor. She'd been foolish again today. She needed to sort her shit out, or she was going to get herself noticed by human authorities, and then what would she do?

She climbed into the shower and startled back at the heat of the water. What had Ben said about the heat? Turn the lever up to make it hotter, so if she turned it down...there. Skin temperature at last. Why did humans find it necessary to boil themselves? And what did they use instead of sand when they wanted to scrub off the dead skin? She poked around, eventually finding a rough, thick cloth of some sort which abraded her skin well enough.

Her hair was another matter entirely. She tugged her fingers through it and nearly wept as they tangled up in limp, unresponsive strands. She missed the way her hair would respond to her emotions or to chemicals and vibrations in the water, how it would move by itself to correct the worst of the tangles. She had no idea how to deal with these dead things now sprouting from her head. If she cut it, would it return if she got home?

When she got home. She had to believe it would happen. She had to keep trying. But she'd tried so hard, and she was running out of ideas. She'd wondered if there was a particular place she had to go to jump into the sea, if it was the location that mattered. She must have tried every damn rock from the beach hut to the muddy cliffs, at every time of day or night, and still, no luck.

Jumping in where the River Esk mixed with the sea had been a last-ditch attempt, hoping that the water there would make the difference. Or maybe the height of the jump. But why would it? She might not have been on land in years, but she surely would have remembered having to jump off those piers.

Even trying to remember what they'd done last time was pointless. Amber had cast a spell on her rather than using an amulet like they always did when they came on land to trade with the select humans who didn't ask questions about where they'd found their polished shells and gemstones. Who knew whether it worked the same way anyway? The amulets were probably a different sort of magic.

Not that Jet would know *that* either way because she had always been too impatient to learn the bloody mage language.

She turned the water off and dried herself on a towel that was much softer and fluffier than the one in the beach hut. It smelled a whole lot nicer too. She should probably find out about towel care if she was going to be stuck here much longer.

She was *not* going to be stuck here. She was going to find her way home.

The clothes Tessa had lent her were warm and stretchy. A good thing, that, because the human was terribly thin, at least by mermaid standards. The stretchy grey trousers were cinched in at the ankles, which was useful as they were a bit long. The black shirt clung uncomfortably around her breasts and shoulders, but it allowed an excellent range of motion. She'd definitely be able to put her armour on over this and have nothing in the way of a good fight.

She gathered her wet clothes into a bundle and padded downstairs barefoot. Tessa nearly bumped into her at the bottom, and her skin turned an interesting pink colour as she looked up. "Hi. Uh. Sorry, I wasn't looking where I was going. Do you want me to put your stuff in the machine?"

"Machine?"

"The washer-dryer." She gestured over her shoulder with her thumb. "I'll put my own stuff in once I've had a shower too."

Jet nodded and handed her clothes over, though she didn't really know what Tessa was talking about. She did notice Tessa's eyes flicker down to map out the shape of her, and she couldn't help but smirk when Tessa's face went even pinker. "Right, clothes, shower, yes. Uh, Ben's in there," she said and all but ran away.

Ben was, indeed, in the kitchen. "Do you want tea? I'm good at making it. I had to write instructions for it for school, and I got a star because I said you should always put a biscuit with it, and my teacher agreed."

"I'd love some tea," she said, amused.

Ben explained the whole process as he went, and Jet didn't bother telling him that her beach hut had a kettle and tea bags already. She'd never tried milk in tea, though, and had certainly not had a custard cream on the side, so the kid did seem to know what he was doing.

"Tessa said we can make pasta for tea when she's done with her shower," he said, leading Jet into the living room and curling up on the carpet. He leaned over a low coffee table to finish his own half-drunk cup.

"Pasta tea?" Jet frowned.

Ben laughed. "Daddy says it's supper, but that's because he's a southerner. There's tea the drink and tea the meal."

"That's confusing," she said with a frown. It did, come to think of it, explain a few things. Humans, living out of the water as they did, needed to drink. Why they decided to call one of their drinks the same as the evening meal was beyond her.

Tessa came downstairs brushing her short blond hair, a small towel draped over her shoulders. "Everyone okay? I'll get tea started now if you're both happy with pasta and bacon."

Ben gave her two thumbs-up. "Can I watch some telly?"

"Please?"

"Please," he said, drawing the word out and clasping his hands under his chin.

"Go on, then."

Jet let Ben chat to her about the TV show he was turning on, and when he'd become engrossed, she slipped out. She had to confront Tessa sooner rather than later.

Tessa turned as she came into the kitchen and jumped and squeaked as she saw her. "God, you scared the crap out of me."

"Who else have you told about last night?" she said, her voice low as she moved closer.

Tessa took a half step backward, her hand catching the counter. "What? Nobody."

"What about those other people you were with? You told them nothing?"

Tessa frowned and shook her head. "Wait, what do you think I would have said?"

"You know damn well what I'm talking about, human."

Tessa looked at her flatly. "You think I've gone around telling people we had a drunken conversation about mermaids? No. No, I haven't told anyone."

Jet closed her eyes and let out a breath. "You need to keep it that way, you hear?"

"Excuse you?"

Jet twisted her lips. She didn't want to threaten. Tessa had been nothing but kind. But she couldn't risk her family, not when she'd put them all in this much danger already. "What will it take to buy your silence?"

"You don't need to buy my silence." She sounded offended. "Look, can I get one thing straight? You really think you're a mermaid?"

"I am a mermaid."

"Mermaids aren't real, though, you said yourself."

Jet snorted. "That's not what you said last night."

"I was drunk *and* high last night. Of course I believed in mermaids."

Jet tilted her head on one side. "Well. That's easy, then. You really aren't going to tell anyone about me?"

Tessa hesitated. "I'm not going to promise that."

"What?"

"I'm worried about you. You say you're a mermaid, and you jumped off a bloody pier. I should be getting you some sort of psychiatric help."

"Do I look crazy to you?"

Tessa snorted and turned back to the chicken she was cutting up. "Yeah, that's not how mental health works."

Jet folded her arms and leaned back against the counter so she could keep an eye on Tessa's expressions. "Go ahead, ask me anything you like. I'll answer, if only to prove to you that I'm not hallucinating or having a psychotic episode or whatever it is you think."

Tessa laughed. It sounded rather humourless. "Firstly, I'm not qualified to make those sorts of judgements. Secondly, are you trying to convince me that you *are* a mermaid? Or that I shouldn't tell anyone you're a mermaid? Because you sound a little bit like you're arguing at cross-purposes there."

Jet glared at her, flustered. "Hey, I could have convinced you that you'd imagined the whole conversation."

"Wow, well done for not gaslighting me. I guess I should be grateful for that?"

"You should, actually. My people have kept their existence a secret for centuries, and I won't let my stupid decisions put them in danger." Not again, she thought, the taste of the memory sour in the back of her mind.

Out of the corner of her eye, she saw Tessa consider her for a moment. "Tell me?"

She wavered. "You swear not to tell anyone about them?"

"I promise." She chuckled. "It's an easy promise to make. Nobody would believe me anyway."

"You still don't believe me, do you?" Jet nudged her with an elbow.

Tessa shrugged. "Sorry, no. Does that bother you?"

"Not at all. It just proves that our methods work. But what do you get out of hearing stories you don't believe?"

"Nothing, I suppose." She paused a moment. "I imagine anything you do tell me, whether it's true or some sort of story, it'll have some grain of reality in it. I guess I'll learn something about you either way."

Jet thought about that and nodded. "Very well. What do you want to hear?"

"What do you want to tell me? What's the first thing that comes to mind when you think about your home?"

"The people," she said promptly. "My mam's the chief, you know?"

"I did not," Tessa said, gently teasing.

"Well, she is. Chief of the Farn Deeps clan, that's our group. There's about three hundred of us living in the cavern system our ancestors built, sunk into the soft ground of the North Sea due east of here."

"There's so few of you."

"There are other clans around," she said. "But there have always been lots more humans. That's why we keep our existence a secret."

Tessa nodded. "I don't blame you. Humans are bastards."

"You say that as if you aren't one."

She snorted. "Ask anyone you like, it's well-known. We're making an utter mess of the planet, and everyone's in denial about how it's going to affect all of us." She dumped the chicken into the pan, and it sizzled almost as angrily as her. "Of course, it doesn't matter to the policy makers because it always affects the poorest in society first. They're all well above the waterline. Bastards."

Jet apprised her anew. "You're quite the warrior, aren't you?"

"Who, me? God, no."

"You may not have the techniques, but you've got the passion. If you were one of my clan, I'd train you to use a spear or sword. You're tall enough to deal with the length of them."

Tessa laughed, her head tilted back. It crinkled the corners of her eyes, and Jet found she couldn't look away. "I can't imagine you with a sword or a spear," she said.

It took a moment for the meaning of the words to sink in, and when they did, Jet was a little insulted. "What's that supposed to mean? I'm bloody good with a spear."

"You have a spear?" gasped Ben from the doorway, and Jet's eyes widened in horror. How had she managed to be so foolish, letting a second human in as many days find out about her?

It was Tessa who saved her. "Jet's pretending she's really a mermaid," she said, winking at the little boy.

"Yes," said Jet quickly. "It's all pretend. Not real." Tessa raised her eyebrows and looked way too amused. "Tessa's a mermaid too," said Jet quickly. "Her tail's...golden. To match her hair."

Tessa's cheeks flushed bright red, but Ben was jumping up and down. "Do me, do me, please. I want to be a mermaid too."

"You'd be a merman if you're a boy," Jet said. "And your tail would be...blue. Like your skateboard."

"Awesome. What colour's your tail?"

"It's black but not a flat boring black like the Knarr chief's tail. It's shimmery, and you can catch glimpses of blue and green if the sunlight hits it."

"Like a magpie's wings," Tessa said, glancing over with a smile.

"What's a *nar*, and why do they have boring tails?"

"Knarr are another clan of mer, they live up in the north," Jet said. "They're like, the bad guys. Their tails are usually much more boring than ours. The hunters often have tails that look like killer whales, you know? Black with white patches?"

"Not gonna lie, that sounds pretty cool," said Tessa.

Jet gasped. "Knarr sympathiser. Ben, your auntie's a traitor. I think we're going to have to fight her."

"You'd better not. I'm making your dinner."

Someone slapped a hand on the kitchen window, and Tessa yelped. Jet actually reached back over her shoulder for her spear before remembering where she was. "Aunt Joanie," Ben yelled and ran to the front door.

"Jesus, Joan, you scared the shit out of me," Tessa said, breathless, leaning on the counter.

A young woman with long blond hair and startlingly blue eyes bounced in with a wicked cackle. "You should've seen your face, Tess." She glanced over at Jet. "Hiya, I'm Joanie, Tess's sister."

Jet waved awkwardly. "I guessed."

"You're early, Joan, I wasn't expecting you till eight. We're about to have tea."

"Yeah, I figured. You got extras for your poor, starving little sister?" Tessa rolled her eyes, and Joanie clasped her hands in front of her face, leaning against Tessa's shoulder. "Please, ma'am? Just the crumbs from your table? I'm a poor orphan child."

"Shut it, you," said Tessa, shoving Joanie's face. "Go set the table, then."

"Ben, set the table, will you?" Joanie said, stealing a piece of chicken right out of the pan with her long, painted nails. Tessa swatted at her hand, and Joanie danced out of the way.

"So," she said, sliding along the counter next to Jet. "Tessa finally got a girlfriend, then?"

"Joanie!" Tessa whipped her head around to stare, her cheeks flushing again.

"What? Have you?"

"You don't *out* me like that. Christ on a bike, what if I'd been keeping it a secret from her?"

"Oh, what, like you do with literally everyone else?"

"It's none of your business who I tell. It's *my* life. And you don't have to deal with it when people are…you know."

Joanie gestured at Jet with a thumb. "What, your gaydar isn't pinging around her? She's not gonna be homophobic. Are you?" she asked Jet. "Nothing straight about you, is there, duck?"

Tessa put her face in her hands and dropped her head to the counter, moaning unintelligibly.

"Huh?" Jet said very eloquently.

"Are you as gay as my sister is or not?"

"I don't know how gay your sister is," Jet said, frowning. She glanced at Tessa, wishing she'd give her a signal, some sort of permission to pick the human up and dump her outside the door. She wouldn't even hurt her. Much. But surely, Tessa would do that herself if she was really upset. Jet sure wouldn't like anyone to fight her battles for her, but would Tessa? Would she want to be protected?

Joanie looked unbearably smug. "Very gay."

Jet crossed her arms. At least she could do this, show some sort of solidarity. "Well, then, yes."

"See?" Joanie said to Tessa, who was now kneeling on the floor with her hands still over her face. "Told you. Gaydar."

"Do all sisters torment each other the way you do Tessa?" Jet asked. Was this a human thing? Or a Joanie thing?

"Probably," said Joanie with a crooked smile. Well. At least she didn't seem homophobic, so that was one thing.

"No," yelled Tessa, muffled by her hands. "You're like Azula from *Avatar* levels of sisterly torment."

"Aw, Tess, you say the nicest things," Joanie said, pressing her hand to her chest.

"Just. Shut up and sit down. Dinner's ready." Tessa stood and caught Jet's eye before flicking her gaze away. "Sorry about her. She isn't…" She sighed. "Just sorry."

"You don't have to be," said Jet. She had the urge to touch Tessa's shoulder, give some sort of comfort, stop Tessa's gaze from flickering around and avoiding everyone. She wanted the old dynamic back, where the teasing seemed to go both ways.

Keep out of it, she reminded herself. It wasn't her battle or her family or her place. She gritted her teeth and sat at the tiny, rickety table.

"Are you going to come out with me tonight, Tess?" Joanie asked as Tessa brought over bowls of pasta.

Tessa shook her head. "Not tonight. I'm knackered."

Joanie rolled her eyes. "You're always knackered. If you're not careful, you'll get old before your time."

"I went out last night, actually," Tessa snapped.

Joanie looked skeptical. "Was it for work?"

"Well, not exactly."

Joanie looked over, the sort of look that invited agreement, invited Jet to be on her side. It set Jet's nerves on edge. "Who did you go out with, Tess? Was it people from work?"

"Well, yeah, but—"

"I knew it," Joanie said in a singsong voice.

"They invited me. As a *birthday* celebration," Tessa said through clenched teeth.

"Because you didn't organise a celebration? You know, one where you invite friends and family and stuff?"

"No, that's not—" Tessa cut herself off, visibly holding her tongue.

"Oh yeah, I forgot. You don't *have* any real friends."

"That's enough," said Jet, voice like a whip crack. The table was silent. Tessa poked at her food, then stood, mumbling something, and disappeared upstairs.

"Shit," said Joanie under her breath. She rubbed her eyes. "I'll go talk to her."

Jet gripped her wrist, and the girl looked at her, eyes wide and showing her youth. "Not if you're going to be cruel again."

Joanie nodded. "I know I went too far. I won't...I'll say sorry."

Jet narrowed her eyes, then let go. Joanie stood, opened her mouth, then shook her head and left.

Jet didn't know if she'd overstepped. Family was a difficult thing. She couldn't bear to see cruelty like that, and she was sure it *was* cruel; that had to be going beyond healthy sisterly dynamics. But maybe she'd have some apologising to do herself. For now, there was a child left behind by the adult stuff. "You okay?" she asked Ben.

He shrugged. "I guess."

They ate in silence for a bit, or in Ben's case, pushed pieces of pasta around his bowl. Poor kid. It was different for a mer. Their communities were small and tight-knit, and for the most part, they ate in large groups. Even if there was adult drama going on, the kids always knew they had somewhere to get away from it. The Farn Deeps clan didn't even have doors. Which, yes, had its own disadvantages. But Jet didn't think she'd ever understand the way humans lived, with rooms and lives closed off from each other.

She put her cutlery down. "Want me to teach you how to use a spear?"

CHAPTER FIVE

Tessa did not allow herself to slam the door behind her. She closed it quietly, picked up a pillow, and screamed into it. She could feel the impotent, furious tears prickling at her eyes, leaking out, and dampening the material. At least it was better than yelling at someone, at hurting them. She couldn't do that again; she couldn't be that angry, grieving teenager anymore. She had to be better.

She paced up and down her room, the conversation replaying in her mind, only this time, she reacted differently. She flipped the table or screamed at Joanie to get out or called her cruel names. Each scenario ended in tears. Usually Ben's.

There was a little knock. "Tess?" Joanie's voice, distorted slightly, as if she was standing too close to the door. "I'm sorry."

Tessa sat on her bed, her back against the wall by the door and hugged her pillow to her chest. She wanted to dig her fingernails into it and tear it apart, feathers flying everywhere.

"Can I come in?"

She let her head drop back against the wall with a *thunk* and closed her eyes. Just for a moment. Then leaned over and opened the door.

Joanie sidled in, giving her puppy eyes. "Hey."

"Hi."

"I'm really sorry, Tess." She sat on the bed next to Tessa, her knees bent up, body turned toward her.

"I know. It's fine."

It wasn't fine. It was infuriating. Joanie was the rebel, the black sheep of the family, the one who partied too much and had been going out and getting drunk since she was fifteen. She said mean things and flaked out on everything, but that was *just Joanie*. People shook their heads and accepted it, and because there was already one tearaway in the family, Tessa couldn't do any of those things.

Joanie poked her in the arm with one long nail. "Are you gonna forgive me?"

"Are you gonna stop?" She bit down on the flood of words, stopped them from drowning everyone.

"I will," Joanie said. "Tess, I *will*. I'm sorry. I mean, I'm not going to stop teasing you. You wouldn't want me to. It'd be boring, right? But I shouldn't have said that about your friends. I won't say it again."

Tessa clenched her jaw once, twice, then nodded, still not looking at Joanie.

"I *won't*."

Tessa sighed and rolled her head to look at her. She was uncharacteristically serious. Tessa wanted to trust her or at least believe this one thing. "Good," she said. "Don't."

Joanie grinned, but Tessa didn't miss the little puff of relief before she slapped the carefree mask back on. "Come finish your dinner, then. With your guardian angel." She waggled her eyebrows.

"What are you talking about?"

"Jet," said Joanie, tugging Tessa to her feet. "She jumped right to your defence, did you hear? I thought she was going to fight for your honour."

Tessa snorted. "Yeah, she wanted you to shut up."

"Admit it, you've pulled."

"Oh my God, I have not."

"You're blushing, you like her." Joanie poked Tessa's cheek, and she slapped her hand away. "Tessa's got a *girlfriend*."

"What are you, twelve?"

They bickered all the way down the stairs, walked into the kitchen, and stopped.

Jet and Ben stood and whipped their hands behind their backs as if Tessa had somehow missed the fact that they'd been fighting with a dusty roll of wrapping paper and a couple of wooden spoons taped together.

"Where did you even find that?" Tessa asked, pointing at the wrapping paper. Of all the questions she had jostling for position, that was the one her brain had spat out at her.

Ben looked at it as if he was considering saying, "How did that get in my hand?" He finally settled on the truth. "Um. Under the sofa."

Joanie put her hands up. "I'm not even gonna ask. You ready to go home, Ben?"

He looked at his watch. "Aw, but Jet was going to teach me how to disarm someone."

"Your mum'll disarm me if I don't get you home in time," said Joanie. "Come on, get in the car."

Ben did that thing that came naturally to every child, drooping his arms and slumping as if he was being taken to his own execution. "Bye, Jet."

"Nice to meet you." Jet did a fancy-looking spin with her wooden spoon spear. The effect was slightly ruined when she went to put it in a scabbard that wasn't there, and it clattered to the ground. She scrambled to pick it up.

Joanie smirked at Tessa like that was somehow meant to impart some meaning. Tessa decided, as usual, to ignore her. "Sure I can't tempt you clubbing?" said Joanie as Ben gathered his things.

"I'm sure."

"I can still crash in your spare room, though, right?"

"As if I could stop you. You've got your key?"

"Duh." She dangled her keyring in Tessa's face. "Don't wait up."

"Never do."

Ben grabbed her by the waist on the way down the corridor. "Thank you for having me."

"Any time," she said, stroking his hair. "Got your skateboard?"

"It's by the door. Jet, are you going to be here again? I've got some wooden swords at home from when I was a little kid. I can bring them for next time."

Jet looked panicked.

"Leave Jet alone, Ben, we only just met her," said Tessa. Ben crinkled up his eyebrows as if that was completely irrelevant. "Go on, see you in a couple of weeks."

The house was always silent whenever Ben left. In that moment after Tessa closed the door and before she turned around, the quiet seemed like a living presence, almost loud in her ears.

This time, Jet shuffled her feet, cutting through it, lifting the pressure. Tessa turned with a sheepish smile. "Sorry about dinner," she said. "And thanks for entertaining Ben."

"My pleasure." She held up the wooden spoons. "I hope you don't mind..."

Tessa laughed. "No, I don't mind."

"Are you okay? I hope I didn't overstep with Joanie. I'm sure you can fight your own battles, I just...really didn't like the way she was talking to you. I'm sorry for butting in."

She shrugged, something unsteady in her chest, pleased and anxious and confused all at once. "I'm fine. Joanie's just like that. Thank you, though. For, well, for defending me, I guess." She laughed. "But it's fine."

Jet watched her for a beat, then nodded, and now the quiet crept in again, different to before. Like Tessa was focused on Jet to the exclusion of everything else, the world holding its breath rather than pushing at her.

The washer beeped, and they both startled. Tessa laughed at herself. "That'll be your clothes."

She pulled them out of the dryer, her clothes and Jet's mixed with the towels from the old couple on the pier, and it came back to her. That she'd known Jet for less than twenty-four hours. She'd comforted her drunk, and she'd jumped into the sea in a failed effort to save her. Was Jet now going to disappear from her life the same way she'd entered?

She tried to brush the melancholy off while handing over a pile of warm, dry clothes. "Will you be heading home tonight? Wherever that is?"

Jet snorted. "I'd like to get home, but as we've both seen, that doesn't seem to be working out for me." She waved the clothes as evidence, then frowned at them. "These are *warm*."

"Washer-dryers are a massive indulgence. I'd choose them over a dishwasher any day."

Jet pressed her face into the clothes, closing her eyes and wrapping the fabric around her cheeks. Tessa couldn't look away. There was something so *sweet* about it.

She didn't want her to disappear.

"Hey, so, you've got to get back to your beach hut, right? Pick up some stuff before you get going? I'll walk you down if you like." She didn't look at her, picked at a loose thread on her own armful of clothes.

"That'd be great," Jet said, and Tessa's heart did a double thump. "I don't know if I'd find my way back otherwise."

Well, that was sensible, she supposed. "Sure, yeah. Give me a minute, I'll get some socks and a jumper."

"Okay. I should probably change, give you your clothes back."

Tessa was a few steps up toward her bedroom as the thought hit her. "Keep them," she said, her voice slightly strangled. It was stupid, and probably a bit weird, but the sight of Jet in Tessa's clothes was…and the shirt fit her so *well*. She'd never be able to wear that shirt again without feeling jealous of it, of the way it'd been hugging Jet.

"Are you sure? This shirt is a fantastic material. It'd be perfect under my armour." She tugged the sleeve down and pinched the material between her thumb and two fingers, tugging the neckline slightly lower.

Tessa's gulp must have been audible. She looked away quickly. "Yeah, of course. It's only Primark's finest."

Jet nodded seriously. "That's very generous of you. Thank you."

Tessa laughed and shook her head, running up to her room to get socks and hoodies. She dropped to sit about halfway back down, handing one pair of socks and a zip-up hoodie to Jet. "For the walk back."

"Oh, you didn't have to."

"It'll be cold. It's fine, really."

"That's very—"

"Wait," Tessa said, the full content of the conversation filtering through to her brain now that Jet's breasts were tragically covered up. "Did you say *armour*?"

"Of course. You know I use a spear. Offense is nothing without a good defense. It's back in the beach hut. I was wearing it when…you know."

Tessa looked at her blankly, still processing the idea of a *real* spear and armour.

Jet caught her look. "You know," she prodded. "When Amber cast me out? The magic that turned me human?" She put her fists on her hips. "Are we going to have this discussion every time I mention my home or being a mermaid? Because that's going to get boring."

Tessa opened and shut her mouth, then gave up and pressed her face into her hands, massaging her eyes with her fingertips. "I can't…mermaids aren't real."

"Sure," Jet said. "Right."

Tessa looked up at her. Her jaw was set, and she was pulling her socks on with harsh, jerky movements. Tessa sighed. "How can I believe without proof? When logically, it makes more sense for you to be making this up or for it to be, I don't know, a hallucination? Some trauma that your mind can't cope with, so it's telling you something different to give you the distance to process it?"

Jet leaned against the wall, the tension leaving her body and making her wilt. "I don't know what proof I can give you. My armour and spear, though I'm sure you could say that they're fakes. My story, my obliviousness to certain bits of human life, all of that can be dismissed more easily. I get it, I do. You barely know me, why would you believe me?"

"It's not that," Tessa admitted. "You jumped off a pier into rough seas. I was scared for you, you know? I've…" She took a deep breath. "I've been there. I've considered jumping myself. Well, not jumping, exactly. It was pills for me. But I've been standing at that precipice, and I don't want to leave anyone else there." She swallowed the memories of darkness, slogging through a thick tar while the world around her walked on dry land, not noticing.

"Are you talking about suicide?" Jet asked, soft and hesitant. Tessa nodded. Jet took a deep breath, and for the first time since Tessa had known her, looked out of her depth. "I don't really understand. I can see it's something very hard for you, and it must have been awful, I'm sorry. But I've never been there. I don't want to die. I want to fight and protect my people, and I can't imagine ever getting to the point where I'm not trying to get home. I'm not suicidal. I promise."

Tessa nodded and tried not to feel torn open, like her heart and all her soft weak places were exposed. "At least promise me you'll call the Samaritans if you ever do, okay?"

Jet bit her lip. "I don't know what that is. And I don't have a phone."

Tessa laughed hopelessly and rubbed her forehead. "It's fine. I'll write their number down for you." She held her own phone up. "I've still got them saved," she said sheepishly. "You can call from a pay phone or something, just promise, okay?"

"I promise," she said.

Tessa looked at her, trying to see past the concerned, open expression. Was it too innocent? Was there something more, something she was missing?

Had she done enough?

Jet smiled knowingly at the scrutiny and held out a hand to pull Tessa up. "I promise, Tessa. If I ever get to that point, I'll call them. But it won't get there, okay? I'm fine."

Tessa mustered up a smile and took her hand, letting her pull her up. "Okay," she said. She sniffed. "Onward, then."

CHAPTER SIX

The lampposts cast a yellow haze over the night as they made their way down Upgang Lane, car tires hissing on the damp tarmac. They walked for a while in silence. At first, Jet felt the quiet between them like a mistake, and she battled to find words that didn't make everything worse. She had never had to deal with concerns like Tessa's, and there was a part of her that longed to take those concerns away, somehow make it all better and shelter her from this pain that still hovered over her shoulders. But even she knew that wasn't how that kind of pain worked.

She watched the white puff of her own breath, tipping her head right back to watch it spiral up into the hazy night. Sometimes, back at home, she'd rise to the surface and take in a lungful of air, then dive back down to blow out a stream of bubbles. They'd float up like this, only much faster, accelerating as the pressure changed and let the air take up more and more space. Here on land, the wind caught the plume of condensation, and it became another part of the damp in the air.

Tessa tugged her hoodie over her short hair. "Weird weather, isn't it? Mizzle soaks you faster than a downpour."

Jet laughed. "Mizzle? Mist and drizzle?"

"Yep."

"You humans really do have a hundred words for rain."

It was Tessa's turn to laugh, and Jet's eyes lingered on her, cataloging the way her nose crinkled and how she tipped her head back a little. "I think that's just the British," said Tessa. "That's what happens when you get this many different types of weather."

Jet tore her gaze away and cast her mind back to home. "We don't get much variation in weather. Temperatures change slower in the water than they do on land, and we have a bit of a delay, so when you guys are coming out of summer, our water's just warming up."

Tessa nodded. "I know some swimmers who say the same. They keep telling me it's warmer to go swimming in November than in August. I don't believe them."

"They're right, but you have to get back out of the water, and in August, you'll warm up quicker, won't you?"

"Exactly what I said. I don't fancy being an icicle. Walking to work's bad enough in the winter without trying to change out of a wetsuit or something daft."

"You work in the town, then?"

Tessa nodded. "Those people I was with last night, they were my workmates. My boss Andy and my team. We're environmental consultants."

"Sorry, I don't know what that is."

She gave a wry smile. "Don't worry, everyone asks. We meet with companies and try to work out ways for them to be more sustainable. Using starch-based packaging rather than plastic or sourcing things from within the UK rather than overseas. Lots of places want to be greener, for whatever reason, but they don't know how. Or they listen to the news and still think that veganism is the only answer to climate change, when actually, sourcing soya from Brazil can be contributing to deforestation in a very delicate ecosystem. Eating British free-range meat is much more sustainable. Lots of farmland here can't be used for anything other than grazing animals and…" She cut herself off and cleared her throat. "Uh. Sorry, got a little carried away there."

"Not at all," Jet said with a frown. "I don't know anything about farm animals, so this is all really useful information. What were you going to say about the grazing animals?"

Tessa stopped and looked at Jet as if she'd given her a handful of pearls. "What, really? You don't mind?"

"Of course not. Why would I?"

She tucked a strand of hair behind her ear. It fell back out again, landing in a smooth curve just below her jawline. "Most people get bored when I start going on a rant about food miles or renewable energy or something. Hannah says I'm a workaholic, but this stuff really matters to me. I feel like I'm doing something that makes a difference, you know?"

"Well, you are, aren't you? Climate change is something that's affecting all of us. We're going to have to dramatically change the way we live if we want to survive. That's why we moved to the old underground caverns in the fifties."

Her eyes widened. "You've made changes like that already?"

She shrugged. "Like you said, our community is tiny. When we find things like this out, we've only got a small number of people to convince that change is necessary. Your society…it's impossibly big and interconnected. We can't even get our heads around it. Well, Amber has to, being a mage."

"Why so?"

"A mage is usually the main liaison between humans and mer. She has to know more about what makes you lot tick so she can set up trade."

They began walking again, Tessa frowning at her feet as they went. "You know, all this logistical cultural stuff is the most convincing part of the whole mermaid thing. I don't know what that says about me."

Jet snorted. "That you're sensible?"

"Only on the surface. Underneath, I'm a hot mess." She stopped as they reached the terrace across the road from the beachfront. "I didn't ask, where's your beach hut?"

Jet led her down the zig-zagging path cut into the side of the grassy cliff. The tide was low, white breakers visible down a long stretch of beach. She stopped as they reached the path lined with beach huts and leaned on the railing to breathe. The wind coming straight toward them from the ocean smelled of home. As close as it could get while still being air, she supposed.

She would get home. She couldn't accept the alternative.

"It's this one," she said, turning away from the siren call of home, so close and yet so far. She took the key out of its hiding place in the eaves of the hut and unlocked the door, dropping her armful of clothes on the counter inside. These would definitely have to be kept separate from those she'd found in the hut and used over the last few days. How had the others managed to clean clothes in the past? There was probably some sort of spell that Amber used. Ugh.

"Wait," said Tessa. "Are you sleeping here?"

"Yes," Jet said, gesturing to the nest she'd made out of blankets and towels. It was quite comfy, actually. "My tribe's owned this beach hut for…well, I suppose since it's existed, so it's got everything we need."

"Yeah, for a day trip," Tessa said, sounding aghast. "These aren't made for living in long-term, Jet."

"I'm not planning to live here long-term. As soon as I find my way home, it'll be locked up again for the next time Mam or Amber comes on land."

Tessa wouldn't stop looking at her like she was about to cry. "Can you just…were you kicked out, Jet?"

"What? No. I said Amber cast a spell on me. There was a fight, and it was getting rough. She needed to get me out of there." She looked down. "Get us *both* out of there, but I don't know…"

Had Amber gotten herself out? Had she managed to get to safety? The last Jet had seen of her, she'd been surrounded by Knarr, and she'd never been much of a fighter. Not like Jet. But she'd sent Jet away, saved her, even though Jet was the one who'd gotten them into that situation. She hadn't left when Amber had asked her to; she should have listened. And now, Amber might be…

"Look, if you need some place to stay, somewhere warmer, I've got a spare room. You can stay there until you get back on your feet."

She could have caused her own cousin's death. And if the Knarr planned to move on Farn Deeps, they could have started doing that. They could have attacked as soon as Jet was gone. Her people could have been ambushed or besieged, and she wouldn't know.

Would she ever know?

"Or if you don't want to stay with me because I'm basically a stranger, I get that, we could find you a shelter or something? I could—"

"Don't," Jet snapped. She couldn't deal with the sad eyes, the *kindness*. It couldn't be aimed at her because she didn't need it because nothing was wrong. Her people were fine. Amber had another spell at hand, and as soon as Jet was out of the way, she'd have sent out a blast and gotten rid of the problem at the source. She was powerful. She was *fine*.

"Sorry," said Tessa.

"I'm fine here," Jet said. "It's my place, it's warm and comfortable, and I don't need your pity." She spat the word and almost immediately regretted it as Tessa stepped back, but Tessa wasn't the important thing. The important thing was getting home, making sure she hadn't ruined everything. Doomed everyone.

"Right," said Tessa. "Right, okay. I'll leave you to it, then." She hesitated and turned at the door, gave an aborted wave, and left.

Jet closed her eyes and told herself she didn't want to run out and call Tessa back.

CHAPTER SEVEN

Sunday felt like a whole different kind of hangover. Tessa lay in bed and stared out the window and tried to pretend that life wasn't a constant minefield.

At some point in her drifting, Joanie shuffled into her room, eyes still shut and crusty with last night's makeup, and flopped onto Tessa's bed. Tessa moved up wordlessly, letting Joanie crawl under the covers and lie on her outstretched arm, her face pressed into the crook of Tessa's neck. "Good night?"

Joanie grunted and reached up, splatting a hand over Tessa's mouth. She laughed softly and took the hint.

She must have fallen back asleep because when she opened her eyes next, the shower was running, and Joanie was singing along to the waterproof radio. The kettle was still warm, and Joanie hadn't finished the last of the coffee, so Tessa took her small wins.

"You going to come see Dad today?" she asked when Joanie emerged and started laying her makeup out on the kitchen table.

"Why bother?" She tried to make it flippant, but Tessa could hear the thread of pain under the defiance.

She patted Joanie's shoulder on her way past to get her socks. "Let me know if you change your mind."

She was halfway up the stairs when Joanie called, "Give him my love, won't you? Just if he's having a good day, you know."

"Of course."

Joanie was gone by the time she came back down. Tessa didn't let herself think about that or about Dad or about Jet and her sudden mood swing and the fact that she'd been sleeping on a nest of towels on the floor of a bloody beach hut. She just drove.

The beech trees outside the care home were already wearing their autumn colours, the leaves in the shade getting tints of red or yellow shooting through them. As Tessa walked in, she saw that a few were already starting to fall.

The receptionist looked up as she approached the desk. "I'm here to visit Tom Bordeaux," she said and tried to convince herself that the receptionist wasn't judging her because she wasn't a regular enough visitor.

"Room 9A," she said. "Do you know where you're going?"

"Yeah, thanks." She didn't bother asking if was a good day or not. No point going in with preconceived notions or anything.

Dad's room faced south, catching the sun and looking over a slightly over-manicured lawn. She thought of the wilderness of their old garden, how she and the others would spend hours playing hide-and-seek when they were really little. Before everything went to shit.

"Dad?" she called, knocking on the open door. "Heya, how you doing?"

He looked up from his newspaper, squinting through his glasses. "Ey-up, lass," he said, and Tessa's treacherous heart leaped with hope. He stood and waved her over for a hug. She could feel the remnants of strength in his arms, and it sent a spike of anger through her. He was too young to be living in an old people's home. "Want a cuppa?"

"Love one. I'll make it," she said. "You got any biscuits to go with it?"

"Yeah, they're in the thing." He frowned. "You know, that thing. On the shelf."

"I'll find them." She filled the kettle and leaned on the counter to open the window. The carers would be around soon enough, and they always closed it, like Dad was an octogenarian or something.

The cupboards were labelled clearly, with pictures alongside words. She remembered Hannah doing the same for Ben when he was little and just starting to read. She'd had them in English and French, of course, because she was a massive overachiever. Ben, to her disappointment, had failed to pick up French.

She drained the teabags from their cups, added sugar to Dad's, and put a few custard creams on a saucer to take in. "On your left," she called as she came back into the living room.

Dad startled. "Scared the living daylights out of me, you did."

"Sorry, Dad."

"Turn the telly on, would you?"

She curled up on the sofa and switched the TV on. The rugby league was playing, and she winced, looking over at Dad, but he chuckled. "You always did love that game, didn't you, Gabe?"

Tessa's heart sank, and she kicked herself for letting herself get complacent. Dad could recognise someone one minute, then call them by a different name the next. The last time Joanie had come had been a really bad day, and halfway through her visit, he'd panicked, thinking there was a complete stranger in his house.

Being called by her dead twin's name was always an extra blow, though.

"How did your last match go? Get any tries?"

She swallowed the lump in her throat. There was no point in correcting him. It only confused and embarrassed him. And then he'd forget in ten minutes' time anyway. "Not this time. I converted one of Billy's, though."

"That's my boy. I'll come to your next game if you let me know the date in good time. Got to ask…"

His voice trailed off. It was both a relief and a horror because it meant Tessa had the mental space to realise that she'd just described Gabe's last match.

Dad spoke a little more, mostly about the Wigan-Leeds match on telly, Tessa assumed. She didn't stay long. Hannah could go screw herself if she wanted to berate her about it. She couldn't stay there with Dad talking to Gabriel through her yet again.

She hated herself when she kissed his cheek good-bye. A coldhearted part of her said that it didn't matter how long she stayed. It wasn't like he'd remember anyway, but who knew? Dementia was unpredictable and horrible, and hadn't they all suffered enough? Hadn't she? Wasn't it enough that she'd walked out basically unscathed from a train crash that had killed her brother and mum? No, the world had to take her dad young too. Not his body but his mind, and in some ways, that was worse. He was still here, she could still hug him and talk to him, but was there really any point when they were all waiting for him to forget them that last time and never say their names again?

She sat in the car for a long time before she could start it up, holding her face in her hands. It all felt fucking pointless. Everything. If all this with Dad was pointless, wasn't it also the case with everyone else? Weren't they all just on a slow but steady decline into oblivion? At times like this, even her job felt hopeless, tilting at windmills. Trying to leave a mark on granite with a fingernail.

❖

"Good morning," said Sophie, practically skipping into the office on Monday morning.

"So it seems." Tessa raised an eyebrow at her.

She blushed. "What can I say? I had a great weekend. How was yours? Get anything nice for your birthday?"

Tessa laughed around the lump in her throat that seemed to have grown. "Both my sisters had a go at me, I tried to save someone from drowning and had to get saved myself, and then my dad mistook me for my dead brother. Fucking fabulous."

There was dead silence, and Tessa realised where she was and who she usually was when she was there. "Oh my God, I'm sorry." She covered her face with both hands. "Please, Sophie, can we forget I said all that?"

"Oh, Tessa, absolutely not," Sophie said. She tugged Tessa's hands down from her face. "Can I please give you a hug?"

Tessa blinked at her. She wanted to reverse time, disappear, set off the fire alarm, anything to keep from facing her own vulnerability. Sophie looked at her with big puppy eyes, her arms stretched out. "Don't feel embarrassed, please? If you don't want a hug, I totally get it, but if it'll make you feel better, I give great ones."

She must have leaned toward Sophie a tiny bit because the kid was wrapping her up in a surprisingly all-encompassing hug. She smelled of aftershave and coffee, and it was so horribly comforting that Tessa had to pull away to wipe her eyes and hide her face. "I'm sorry."

"Don't you dare," said Sophie, and Tessa had to laugh at her indignant tone. "You've had a shitty time of it." She put a hand on Tessa's shoulder and waited until Tessa reluctantly met her gaze. "You're allowed to ask for help, you know?"

"I know," she said because she did, logically. To really get it viscerally was another matter. "There's a time and a place, isn't there? Work is not that place."

Sophie made a *pfft* sound and waved a hand. "We spend such a massive percentage of our life at work, when else do we get the chance to have emotions? While we're sleeping?"

Tessa chuckled and wiped the last tears away. She checked her mascara in the reflection on her phone screen, sniffed and sat up straight, putting herself back together physically in the hopes that the emotional aspect would take care of itself.

"You know we all like you, don't you, Tessa?" Sophie asked, hesitant. Tessa stared. "I mean, all of us...we'd all help you out if you needed it. Even if that means listening to a bit of a rant. We all know you'd do the same for us."

Tessa couldn't say anything to that. Sophie smiled at her, squeezed her shoulder, and went over to her own station to gather her stuff for the weekly meeting.

Chapter Eight

Jet lay curled in her nest in the beach hut until far too late into the day, and by the time she emerged, she had a headache. She sat with her legs hanging off the edge of the path in front of her hut and watched the surf through squinted eyes.

She thought about Saturday night and gritted her teeth, wishing the memories would sod off and leave her in peace. She didn't know how to feel, guilty for pushing Tessa away? Angry at being patronised and not believed? Though she supposed it was a good thing Tessa didn't believe her. It kept her people safe.

She pressed her fingertips to her eye sockets and fought the urge to cry because that was the bottom line, wasn't it? She didn't know if her people were safe. What had the Knarr been planning? They'd obviously settled in that section of the buffer zone, blatantly breaking the accord that had ended the war over thirty years ago. How much further would they go to grab more land? Farn Deeps was well-known for being easy to defend, and with a massive network of caverns deep in the bedrock, stretching farther than even Jet knew, it was pretty much impossible to defeat in a siege. The clan only lived in about a fifth of that space, and though the rest was crumbling and probably unsafe, in the event of an attack, they'd be able to hide or escape through the many tunnels.

But if the Knarr attacked fast enough, if they took out the warriors quickly, and the alarm wasn't raised…

She stood and stamped back into the hut, determined to distract her mind. She couldn't go swimming. Turned out, humans got stressed out if you tried to dive into the sea fully clothed. Having experienced the wonders of a washer-dryer, she wasn't too keen on the feeling of wet clothes after a swim or the salt crusting them up after they dried.

She pulled out her own clothes from where she'd changed when she'd first arrived. They felt alien, though, dry as they were. Mer clothing was designed to be wet all the time, and though her tunic had changed shape into a knee-length dress to cover her human modesty, Jet didn't know if it could withstand the air much longer. The material looked wrinkled, like dried-out seaweed. Maybe, like seaweed, it would benefit from being soaked in the sea.

She crumpled it and put it in a little plastic bucket she'd found on the beach a few days before. Human children seemed obsessed with the things, though they often left them behind when their parents drove away. This one was shaped like a castle and served her well enough as a holdall since she didn't have a bag, and the stash of human money was running worryingly low. Mam and Amber only spent a night in the beach hut at the very most. More often, they'd transform in the early hours of the morning, have a cup of tea and dry off, then run errands and return to the sea late that night. They hadn't planned for things like grocery shopping when they left spending money for the next excursion.

The sun was warm on her back, yesterday's clouds having blown away. The wind remained, still chilly and whipping her hair into more unbearable tangles. She walked barefoot down the beach, just at the wave line, the bucket swinging from one hand. She scooped up some seawater as she walked, letting her tunic soak. The movement rocked the bucket, and water splashed onto her thigh, making patches of cold soak through her rolled up trouser leg.

In another situation, she would be able to appreciate the beauty of the land and the alien culture. Amber had talked her ear off enough about the complex history of the place, after all, to the point where she could recognise Roman settlement sites and houses still standing from centuries ago. As if they didn't have structures that old back in Farn Deeps.

Humans had a way of growing their homes around obstacles, building to follow the shape of the shore, their roads to run alongside rivers, and new buildings side by side with ancient ones. Jet wasn't as much of a fan as Amber was of humans and their cultures, but she did have some respect for what they'd managed to do. Humans were intrusive and chaotic, and far, far too ambitious for their own good, but she could understand their survival instinct.

That was the best she'd ever been able to say for them, but now her mind drifted back to Tessa. She'd always thought of humans as a species, not as a group of individuals. Talking to Tessa, first in the pub and then in her home, she couldn't believe how comfortable she'd been. It was like talking to another mer. She hadn't expected to find such a connection with a human.

She'd certainly never expected to find a human this attractive.

And that was the other thing. What the hell was she doing thinking about some random human she'd just met when she should be trying to find her way home? Jet frowned at the beach, now stonier than it had been when she'd started. She'd wanted to distract herself from worrying about her people, but thinking about Tessa now felt like a betrayal. On top of that, thinking about Tessa wasn't even a comfortable experience because she'd all but yelled at her yesterday when she was only trying to help.

Jet stopped walking. The path ahead was blocked, the tide starting to come in, and a dark sea wall jutting out into the breakers. Beyond that, the beach disappeared, replaced by cliffs. If there was any sand past there, it was now covered by waves. She sighed and turned around and began trudging back.

Somehow, getting back always seemed harder.

CHAPTER NINE

"Tessa, you got a min?"

Tessa turned at the exit to see Elias striding down the hallway. "Sure, what's up?"

"Nothing major, just got a message to pass on." He took his jacket from the coatrack and passed hers along but didn't say anything until they were out in the car park.

"Is everything okay?"

He glanced back, making Tessa's internal alarm bells ring even louder. What could he possibly have to say that shouldn't be heard by anyone else in the company? He must have seen her expression because he huffed a little laugh. "Sorry, I'm not trying to be all mysterious. It really is nothing major."

"Well, you're doing a great job of keeping it low-key," she said. "I feel like a Cold War spy."

He grinned. "It's my partner. You asked for his pronouns on Friday night?"

Tessa covered her face and groaned as the memory returned. "Oh God, I'm sorry, I haven't been that drunk in years."

"Why are you sorry? He appreciated it. That's what I wanted to say."

"It can be invalidating, can't it? I didn't recognise him as a man, so I asked for his pronouns. Ugh, I'm usually much better at working these things out subtly. Please tell him I would never have been that blatant about it if I wasn't full of tequila."

"I suppose that's a point," Elias said thoughtfully. "I hadn't considered that. But you don't have to feel bad. He likes looking androgynous. He doesn't identify as nonbinary, but he likes having long hair and wearing makeup sometimes." Elias shuffled his feet and looked down. "But we both wanted to say that it sort of outs you to us, you know?"

She felt like she'd had cold water poured directly into her veins. "What do you mean?"

He made a face. "Am I wrong about this? God, I'm making a total fucking mess of this conversation, and it was supposed to be, like, extending a hand, you know? We both figured that if anyone asks for someone's pronouns, it's usually because they're in the community." He winced. "Shit. Did I get the wrong end of the stick?"

"No, I…" Tessa closed her eyes and tried to control the adrenaline pulsing through her and telling her that if people *knew*, they'd change, they'd be disappointed, different toward her, and she couldn't stand it if her team changed, but Elias was also…

She swallowed. "I'm gay," she said, and realised that was the first time she'd said that aloud. She was thirty-fucking-two, and she'd never said it aloud, not even when she'd come out to her sisters, not even to her exes. And now she was crying in the car park of her work. Fantastic.

"Do you need a hug?" Elias asked. His voice was very soft, and he was standing hunched and uncertain, a way she'd never seen him. "I'm sorry, Tessa, I didn't mean to upset you."

"It's fine," she said, wiping her eyes. "God, this is the second time I've cried at work, what the hell is wrong with me?"

"Sod that, it's good for you. I cry at sad adverts. A day without crying is a day wasted, I'm sure."

She laughed. "I think I'm doing it wrong, then. All it does for me is give me a headache."

"You just need more practice. Hug's still on offer, by the way, if you want it." He held his arms out with a sheepish smile.

Tessa gave up on professionalism and wrapped her arms around his waist. "There we go," he said, sounding much more like his old, slightly arrogant self. He patted her back before they pulled back. "I really am sorry. Are you that stuck in the closet?"

She laughed. "Yeah, it's a mess in here. Vacuum's fallen over, and it's blocking the door."

"You gotta break that thing down, girl. Emerge like the lesbian butterfly you are."

Tessa was giggling now, bent over with the pull of her stomach muscles. She straightened up and shook her head at him. He was looking almost smug at having made her laugh. "I've been so nervous about coming out here," she admitted and sighed, the seriousness sneaking back in. "Work's important to me, you know? I feel like I belong here. Like I'm doing what I'm *meant* to be doing. I couldn't risk pushing it."

He nodded. "If you don't tell people you're queer, they can't be homophobic about it, huh?"

She nodded. "I couldn't bear it if I wasn't accepted. Not here."

His gaze softened to something awfully like pity, and she considered bristling at it, but he tutted instead. "And then you find out you're not the only gay in the village." He gestured to himself. "Bad luck, Tess. You're not special."

She shoved his arm. "Dickhead."

He gasped. "Such unprofessionalism from our glorious team leader. I'm shocked."

"It's nearly seven p.m. Even I'm off the clock now."

"You want a lift home?"

She shook her head, looking up at the dark sky. "I need to stop by the corner shop. And a walk will do me good, clear my head."

He patted her shoulder. "All right, I'll see you tomorrow. Remember, you're not as alone as you think, okay? I know we're workmates, but we're here for you. Not just for work."

"Thanks," she said softly. She waited a little longer, leaning against the low wall of the parking lot and staring into a sky haloed with streetlights.

She'd felt like she had to do things alone for such a long time. Certainly, all her adult life. But maybe there was still time for that to change.

CHAPTER TEN

Jet had always been stubborn. Mam had moaned about it since as far back as she could remember. So it took her a good few days before she would admit that she couldn't keep waiting for the magic to work or keep trying the same things over and over again in the hope that this time, she'd grow her tail back.

She also had to admit that she only had one person somewhat on her side in this new world, and she might have pushed her too hard. She owed Tessa an apology.

Making the decision had a surprisingly intense effect on her mood. She hadn't realised how guilty she'd felt about snapping at Tessa. She had to admit, she missed her conversation, which was ridiculous after only knowing her for two days.

Even so, she retraced her steps from Saturday night and felt quite smug when she found Tessa's house. Navigating the human world was very different to under the sea, but in some ways, it was easier, if you trained yourself to look at the signs and the landmarks rather than the cardinal directions and the time that had passed.

She didn't seem to have her magnetic sense as a human anyway, so she definitely couldn't use that to find her way. All things considered, she thought she'd done pretty well.

The next problem was that the door was locked. Jet figured that humans might keep their keys in hiding places, similar to how her clan kept the beach hut key when nobody was using it.

She reached up and ran her fingers along the door frame, then started poking through the rocks and plants beside it.

The neighbouring door opened, and she stood with a relieved smile. The elderly woman who appeared was frowning through a narrow gap in her door, a chain still joining the door to the frame. "Are you looking for someone, love?"

"Yes, I wanted to see Tessa."

She nodded. "Is she expecting you?"

Jet made a face. "No, I suppose not."

"And would she be happy about you trying to break into her house?"

Jet blinked. "I wasn't trying to break in, I was looking for the key. I owe her an apology. I wouldn't want to make things worse."

The lady took a deep breath and muttered something like, *young people today*. "Word to the wise, duck. If you're coming to make amends, you wait to be invited in. Don't go invading her space on top of whatever else you've done."

"Huh," Jet said. "Okay. I'll wait on the wall until she gets back. Thank you for the advice."

The old human shook her head and retreated. "Damn crazy millennials," she muttered.

Jet considered taking offence, but she couldn't be bothered. She was tired after a couple of sleepless nights, and hungry too, and running low on cash. She sat on the wall and wondered how long Tessa would be.

Turned out, she was away bloody ages.

Jet had given up on getting comfortable on the wall and instead sat on the doorstep, leaning against her door. She hadn't expected to fall asleep, but the next thing she knew, she was waking up with a start to Tessa kneeling in front of her and shaking her shoulder.

Tessa jerked backward. Understandable. Jet tended to assume that anyone trying to wake her was doing so for nefarious reasons and lashed out.

"Sorry," she said once her brain had connected to the rest of her body again.

"It's fine."

Jet slumped back and rubbed her face with both hands. "I'm also sorry for being rude to you on Saturday."

Tessa's eyes widened. "Oh no, that was my fault. I didn't mean to be patronising, I'm sorry."

She shook her head. "It was more to do with me thinking about my folks back home and getting upset, and I took it out on you."

Tessa held out her hand and hauled Jet up. "Want to come in for some tea?"

"I'd love some."

The next door opened, and the old woman from earlier stuck her nose out through the chained gap. "You all right, Tessa love?"

"Hi, Enid, yes, thanks. Are you?"

"I see you found your friend," she said, somehow jerking her chin at Jet, even while restricted to the small gap. "She was trying to find the key. I wasn't sure if she was a wrong'un."

Tessa laughed and disguised it as a cough. "No, she's fine, thank you."

"Just wanted to make sure you were safe."

"That's really kind of you, thanks, Enid."

"I made some of that cake you like. I'll bring it over later, all right?"

"That would be lovely, thank you very much. I'll see you in a little while, okay?" She shoved Jet inside mid-wave and shut the door behind them. "Sorry, if you let her get talking, we'll be standing out there for hours." She frowned. "Speaking of, how long were you out there waiting?"

Jet looked down at her watch, which didn't work without the currents flowing through and storing power. She shrugged.

Tessa peered at it. "That's not…where did that watch come from? Is it one of those fancy ones that tells you the phases of the moon and all that? God, it must be worth a fortune."

"No, it's not special, just a standard one. Works on a fusion of clockwork and tidal energy, so I don't have to get it charged up every night, which is good. I think you humans have something similar. They charge up from your movement?"

"Kinetic watches, yeah." Tessa stared at her and shook her head. "This is mad." She kicked her shoes off and led the way into the kitchen, flicking on the kettle and getting mugs out of the cupboard, still shaking her head and muttering to herself intermittently.

"Still don't know whether to believe me, do you?"

She sighed and leaned back against the counter, tapping her short fingernails against the laminate surface. "Have you ever heard of Occam's Razor?"

"I don't think so."

"It's usually expressed as the idea that the simplest explanation is most likely to be correct, but that's why I'm struggling here because which explanation is really the simplest? On one hand, you might be making all of this up, maybe as a way for your brain to keep you safe from the pain of reality. You're living in a beach hut and talking about being cast out, and to me, that sounds like…well, like your family found out you were gay and threw you out, so you're sleeping rough."

"My family doesn't care that I'm gay. My dad's bisexual, actually," she said because convincing someone she wasn't imagining something was an exercise in futility.

Tessa blinked, her flow interrupted. "Oh. That's great, I'm glad. But you could also just be telling me that. Telling yourself that, even. After all, we're told from a really young age that mermaids aren't real, that they're a myth based on sailors in the sixteenth century or whatever, watching sea cows suckle their young." Jet burst out laughing. Tessa turned pink and shrugged. "I mean, I don't get that either."

"I honestly don't know who was responsible for that, whether it was us feeding you lot misinformation or you guys making your own weird conclusions."

"Most humans would agree, we're pretty weird."

Jet leaned her chin on her hand. "What's the other explanation, then?"

Tessa poured the tea and passed a cup to Jet before taking a deep breath. "That it's all true. It would explain the fact that you're really good at some human things like speaking English with a Geordie accent and really terrible at others, like apparently thinking it's appropriate to break into my house to apologise to me."

"Humans are really into doors, aren't they?"

"Are mermaids not?"

"Not really. And it's only mermaids if you're talking about feminine mer. Mer, or merfolk, is the collective, gender-neutral term."

"That makes sense."

"Well, then, which is the simplest explanation?" Jet pressed.

"I don't know. They both sound ridiculous, honestly, or equally complicated. One requires a centuries-long conspiracy to hide from humanity, while the other requires you to have the kind of brain that responds to traumatic events by creating complex cover-ups. And that happens, I'm sure, but I'm deeply unequipped for dealing with it."

Jet thought for a moment. "Look at it this way: what can you do about either option?"

"What do you mean?"

"Like you said, you're not a therapist, you can't help me if this is all some creation in my own mind. But if mer do exist and I happen to be a displaced one, can you do anything about that, either?"

"Uh, I don't think so."

"Neither do I. You might as well take me at my word and go from there."

Tessa sat, her gaze distant. "You've got a point."

The silence allowed Jet to think through her own words, and she bit her lip. "You don't have to deal with it at all, of course.

Like you said, you're not equipped to deal with this, and it's certainly not your responsibility. I only came here to apologise. If you want, I could finish my tea and leave with no hard feelings and never see you again."

Tessa looked up, her dark eyes guarded. "Would *you* want that?"

"Honestly, no. But my mam always told me that both people have to want a rel…a *friendship* for it to work. I won't force my presence on you."

"I don't want that. I mean, I don't want you to leave just like that." Her voice was soft, and Jet smiled and told herself that she had specified *friendship* because that was all she wanted from her.

"Then consider me sticking around." Her smile faded. "Not that I seem capable of leaving."

"Is there anything I can do to help?"

Jet sighed and slumped. "I don't know. Usually, when we come on land, we non-mages wear an amulet that allows us to change back into a mer when we're completely submerged in the sea, but this was a spell cast in an emergency. I don't understand enough about either type of magic to know how to fix it."

"What was the emergency?"

"Amber and I, we found a big group of Knarr in the buffer zone."

"Wait, wait. I'm going to need some context there. You mentioned the Knarr before, the ones with black and white tails, right? What's the buffer zone?"

"Yeah, the Knarr are another clan of mer from the northeast. Over toward what you lot call Denmark or Scandinavia, that sort of area. We were at war with them up until a little bit before I was born. My dad got injured. They ripped his lower jaw clean off. He nearly died, I nearly…I nearly grew up without him, and he's such a great guy, I can't imagine what life would've been like. God, the last thing I said to him was that he was being a stubborn arse." She stopped herself and cleared her throat. "The buffer zone is an area between our territory and theirs. Mam and their leader, they made an agreement when the war ended to stay away from each other. And Amber and I found them *living* there."

Tessa leaned her chin on her elbows and watched Jet as if nothing else mattered to her. As if she had all the time in the world to listen but also as if it was okay if Jet didn't want to tell her any more. Jet felt a warmth under her ribs, spreading outward, like Tessa was the sun shining on her.

"We shouldn't have gone as close as we did," she admitted, almost in a whisper. "Amber was trying to convince me to go back, tell Mam and the guards…we weren't even on guard duty. We shouldn't have been patrolling, but I wouldn't be told. So when they saw us, we were surrounded, outnumbered, and alone. Nobody knew where we were." She shook her head. "I tell the youngsters all the time, don't go anywhere unless someone knows where you've gone. I'm such a hypocrite. And Amber might be paying the price."

Tessa covered Jet's fist with one hand, her thumb gently rubbing Jet's healing knuckles. Jet took another deep breath. "Amber's not much of a fighter. I was in front of her to *protect* her. She doesn't even carry a weapon, and her spells always take ages and loads of concentration. They're not *for* battle. But there were more and more Knarr joining the fight, and she cast it at me." Jet flicked her fingers, an insufficient demonstration in every way. "And I appeared on the beach here."

There was silence, just the humming of Tessa's electrical appliances or of the pipes in the wall, Jet couldn't be sure. It wasn't a heavy silence, though. It felt as if Jet had off-loaded a weight, something she hadn't experienced before spending significant time as a human.

"Why do you think she sent you here?" Tessa asked. Her hand was still over Jet's. It felt nice.

"Either because it's the nearest land to where we were or because she knows it well. She and Mam are the ones who come on land most."

Tessa tensed slightly. "Is she your girlfriend?"

"My cousin."

"Oh." Tessa's other fingers tapped a rhythm on the table. "So…how do you usually get back? Mer in general, I mean?"

"Just dive back into the water, which I've tried, obviously."

"Yes, I've been privy to that, thanks."

She rolled her eyes. "Usually, the amulet does it all."

"Yeah, that makes sense." She tap-tapped again. "I don't suppose you could go scuba diving to try to find them? There are places around here where you can hire the equipment."

"I tried," she said. "Mam always made sure we knew what areas to avoid because of divers, so of course Amber and I used to go watch them when we were kids. Turns out, they don't let you hire the gear without some sort of qualification, and the qualification itself is expensive and long. That, and Farn Deeps is nearly three hundred feet down. Apparently, regular scuba gear doesn't go that deep?"

"God, no, it doesn't," said Tessa. "At depths like that, you're talking serious specialist equipment, something to do with oxygen toxicity, I think. Sorry, Jet. I wish I could suggest something, but I wouldn't have the first clue of, like, the rules of magic."

"Honestly, me neither," Jet said with a sigh. "It always took too long and required learning too many fancy words. Give me a spear any day." She tilted her head at Tessa. "You sound like you believe me now."

Tessa considered. "I suppose I'm always going to struggle to believe. We spend years training children *not* to believe in so many things, it's hard to go back on that." She treated Jet to a little smile. "I believe you as much as it's possible for me to do right now. I'm sorry, that probably isn't what you want to hear."

"Not at all." Jet shook her head. "It's honest. What more could I ask for?"

She was looking right at her, which meant she saw the trajectory of Tessa's blush, the pink drifting across her face, before Tessa turned and stood, her hand slipping from Jet's. "I was going to heat up some curry for dinner, would you like some?"

Jet's stomach grumbled loud enough for Tessa to hear and laugh, and maybe it was her turn to blush. "If you've got enough, I'd love some."

"Pass me that Tupperware from the fridge, then, would you? I'll get the plates."

Jet caught herself smiling into the fridge, poking at boxes and bantering with Tessa about humans and their weird names for things. Her body was heavy and longed for the support of water. Her legs hurt, and she missed her sensory hair, not to mention her people, her family. She was far from home.

But here there was food and laughter, a warm kitchen, and Tessa smiling, Tessa tucking her hair behind her ears, Tessa sitting across from her, and somewhere inside Jet's chest, something soft and sweet felt like it was taking root.

CHAPTER ELEVEN

Tessa had intended to play it cool. Jet might have been beautiful and fascinating and friendly, but Tessa wasn't going to give her the chance to find out that she herself was a bit dull. And anyway, maybe Jet was done with her. She'd come to find her and apologise, sure, but that meant they'd had closure, right? They could both move on with their life without baggage.

If anyone was going to continue the friendship, it had to be Jet. Tessa was not going to make herself a burden on anyone. She couldn't bear the thought of Jet becoming bored of her, wishing she'd leave her alone.

Of course, then she saw her in town on her lunch break, and all her plans went out the window as Jet waved wildly. "Tessa," said Jet, her face splitting into a grin as she ran across the street. "I was just thinking about coming to visit you."

"You were?" Tessa felt her cheeks warm in defiance of the chill wind. "I'm going to get some lunch, want some?" She bought baguettes from a corner shop, and they leaned on the sea wall to eat them.

"You're wearing those clothes again, the thin ones," said Jet, tilting her head on one side.

Tessa looked down at her pantsuit. "Thin ones?"

Jet nodded. "On the first day, you had these thick blue trousers. Today and yesterday, it's thin black ones. Don't they tear easily?"

She shrugged. "Compared to jeans, sure, but jeans aren't smart enough for work."

Jet frowned. She looked almost offended. "Surely, work is when you need thick sturdy clothes the most."

"I work in an office," she said, trying to suppress her smile. "Most of the time, I type stuff and have meetings. There's not much wear and tear I have to deal with. And anyway, I'm pretty good at mending." She turned to show the neat blanket stitch holding the pocket together.

"Huh." Jet chewed on her prawn cocktail baguette thoughtfully, then shrugged. "What are you working on at the office today?"

Tessa looked at her food, swallowing her enthusiasm. "Are you sure you want to ask that? I might talk your ear off, and it's probably desperately boring to you."

Jet snorted. "Tessa, I could go back to my beach hut and stare at the sea in the hope that inspiration will strike, or I could listen to you tell me about sustainability and what kind of food is better to buy at this time of year."

"Really?" She didn't want to ask again. Hannah would have said it was attention seeking, fishing for compliments, but she needed to be sure.

In response, Jet hopped onto the wall, crossed her feet at the ankles, and took a big bite of her sandwich, looking at Tessa expectantly.

Tessa laughed softly. "Okay, you asked for it. At the moment, I'm finishing up a bit of invoicing for the food wholesaler we were presenting to last week, and I'm doing some research on the new fisheries legislation. There are some problems with green energy projects like offshore wind farms pushing a lot of fishermen out of their territory, and I'd like to see if I can work out some sort of compromise. See, the fishing industry is seen as archaic and even damaging to the environment by some people, and from what I can tell, a lot of fishermen feel disenfranchised by the government as a whole. I mean, don't we all?" She leaned back against the wall, waving her food as she got into her stride. "But surely, there's got to be some sort of middle ground? After all, sustainability isn't about doing everything one way. There are people whose entire family has been involved in fishing. There's decades of history and tradition and a whole *culture* associated with these boats, and that shouldn't be thrown away. And after all, if we're going to try to save these habitats, make them last longer, it's in the fishermen's interest. And they'd know better than any of us what works and where the wind is strongest, where different fish are found. They're out there every day, after all." She caught herself and stopped. "Sorry. I told you it was boring."

"Don't do that," said Jet, her mouth half-full of food. She swallowed hard and shook her head. "Don't tell me I should find it boring. I don't. It's interesting even when I don't understand all of it, but this, this is stuff to do with the sea. Of course I'm going to find it interesting."

Tessa wrapped her arms around herself, tugging her coat close. It felt a little like she needed something to hold herself together in the face of this unbridled positivity. "I was thinking, I should find myself a fisherman to talk to, get his view on this. Maybe a mermaid would have good perspectives too."

Jet nodded, though Tessa had mostly been joking. "Well, we do collect mussels from your wind turbines. They act like a pretty good reef."

"Huh," said Tessa, and her mind sparked off down a route of research plans, forgetting her embarrassment. "I'll have to look into that." She glanced at her watch. "Shit, I'm going to be late. It was great to see you, Jet, but I've got to go."

"Oh, okay," she said, and Tessa blinked at her audible disappointment. All of a sudden, Jet looked lost.

Tessa bit her lip. Her heartbeat was already picking up at the thought of putting herself out there for rejection, but… "Hey, do you want to meet up after I'm done with work? I can come find you at your hut."

Jet perked up, the wide, crooked smile returning to her face, and Tessa felt her heart stumble, a warning she had no intention of heeding. "That would be great," said Jet.

"Great," she said back, then realised she was the one who should be leaving at this point. "Uh, I'll…" She gestured behind her. "I'll see you later, okay? About five thirty?"

Jet held up her nonfunctional watch. "I'll be there anyway."

Tessa grinned back and turned to go, tucking her half-eaten sandwich back into the paper wrapping and into her deep jacket pockets. She couldn't stop herself smiling on the walk back, the wind cold against her teeth. She was going to see Jet again.

She might even leave work on time.

CHAPTER TWELVE

It was becoming a habit to meet Tessa for lunch, then wait for her on the slope outside the hut as the sun started to make its way down into the sea. Tessa would walk down the beach after work, shoes and socks dangling from her fingers, and wave wildly as soon as she caught sight of Jet. Then they'd sit side by side and talk as they watched the sunset before making their way back to Tessa's house for dinner.

Jet even stayed over in the spare room some days. The bed was odd, too soft and yielding, but she liked the smoothness of the sheets and how she didn't wake up with towel marks all over her skin.

She was getting into a routine, and it was dangerous.

Even more dangerous was Tessa herself. Particularly the little smile Tessa gave as she walked up the slope to Jet's beach hut and sat on the concrete next to her.

"It's Friday," she said in a singsong, holding up a bottle of wine and shaking it. "I thought we'd have fish and chips and drink red wine out of mugs like classy birds."

Jet laughed but jumped up to hook a couple mugs off the table inside the hut. "I don't know what birds have to do with it, but I'm in."

"Slang for women," she said with a shrug, twisting the cap off the bottle and sloshing the wine into the mugs. "It's a bit derogatory. I shouldn't use it really, but I'm British, and I take self-deprecation seriously."

"British and Northern," agreed Jet, tapping her mug against Tessa's. "Not that I'm complaining, not at all, but why is Friday fish, chips, and wine time?"

"It's the weekend," she said with a little amused noise, as if she forgot every few moments that Jet didn't follow the same time patterns as her. "No work for a couple of days. I can be irresponsible for a little."

"Oh, well, if that's the case, I'm always down for an opportunity to be irresponsible."

Tessa looked at her skeptically, and Jet rolled her eyes. "Okay, fine, that's not me at all. But you're one to talk, Miss 'I love my job and enjoy researching new ways to improve the world.'"

Tessa wrinkled her nose, which was unacceptable, really; nobody should be allowed to look that cute while eating greasy chips out of paper and swigging wine from an enamel mug. "Careful, you're going to sound like my sister."

"You take that back." Jet waved a chip at her.

Tessa giggled and leaned against the railing, which wasn't an apology. Jet narrowed her eyes, but the sun had been warm that day, one last whiff of summer baking the ground, and the wind that dusted over them was refreshing. It was too beautiful an evening to feel anything but at peace.

"Did you have a job?" Tessa asked after a moment of soaking up the gentle surf sounds. "I never asked."

"Not in the same way you do," Jet said. "I have responsibilities, though. Mam sets up a rota of patrols in the buffer zone, and I do a bunch of those. Not as many as I'd like." She looked at her hands. "I was fighting with my dad about it before…" She swallowed, and the smell and sound of the sea was overwhelmingly sad, her home so close and so far all at once.

Tessa squeezed her arm. "Do you want to talk about it?"

She cleared her throat and stared back out across the waves. "I was angry because they weren't taking the recent Knarr incursions seriously. I wanted to increase patrols. I was happy to do them myself. I would have been out there every day if that was what it took to keep my people safe." She shook her head. "Amber says I'm always looking for a fight, but I'm not. I'm trying to *avoid* a war, and if that means a short, sharp fight sometimes, then surely, that's worth it, right?"

She glanced over at Tessa, who shrugged. "I suppose that makes sense."

"Right? Anyway, Dad was getting angrier and angrier, telling me I was being stupid, being a warmonger, and I…" She tugged at her hair, shame and anger and resentment bubbling back up. "I've told you he was injured, right? In the war. He can't speak verbally. He talks with his hands, and I…I turned away from him. Just swam off. I know, I *know* it's horrible and disrespectful, and he can't be heard if he can't be seen, so not looking at him is the worst, but I couldn't stand it."

"I get that," Tessa said gently, her hand still on Jet's arm, thumb stroking her bicep.

Jet took a long breath, salt air filling her lungs, stretching them. "Anyway," she said. "I guess that would be my job if I had one. Patrolling." She snorted at herself. "I went off patrolling anyway, you know? That's how I found the Knarr."

"Yeah?"

She nodded. "Amber didn't want to come, but she also wouldn't leave me alone. She heard something and did a searching spell, and that's how we found them. And I keep thinking that if I'd listened to them, on the one hand, I'd still be at home, and I'd know Amber was safe. But on the other, I was the one who found the Knarr. If I hadn't gone out patrolling against orders, they could've been hiding there for God knows how long, plotting."

Tessa kept stroking her arm, keeping her calm gaze on Jet. "Why would they be there in the buffer zone?" she said, a little frown marring her face.

"Oh, not you too." Jet tugged her arm free, embarrassment heating her cheeks. "I thought you believed me."

"I didn't mean that, and you know it," said Tessa. "Don't put words in my mouth."

Jet made a face. "Sorry," she said. Even she was aware it sounded a little mulish. "But why does it matter why they were there? Isn't it obvious?"

"You think they were planning to attack at some point?"

"Of course."

She thought a moment, tapping her chin. "But why now? Why there?"

"Why does it matter? They're the enemy. Tessa, they tore my father's jaw off. I don't care about their feelings."

"I'm not saying you have to," she said. "But knowing someone's motivations can help you predict their next moves, can't it? I mean, I get that I'm not a warrior like you, but the strategy is the same. If I know what motivates someone, I know how to approach them. With money, convenience, patriotism?" She shrugged. "Maybe that makes me manipulative."

Jet frowned and leaned on the railing, staring out to sea in thought. "No, you have a point," she said slowly. "If I know what they want, I can work out where they'll attack first or when or how."

"That's what I'm saying." She nodded. "Bit of research never hurt anyone."

"You're such a nerd," Jet said, and it came out fonder than she had been aiming for. Tessa smiled, oblivious, and refilled their cups. The wind blew strands of hair over her face, the bridge of her nose. Jet wanted to brush it back, tuck it behind her ear, and see how her cheek felt cupped in the hollow of her hand.

She looked away, back out to sea toward home, toward the people who needed her, who might be in danger because of her. Jet couldn't afford to keep falling away from them, falling toward a human, however much she wanted to. Tessa was a distraction, especially when her people could be in trouble. Tessa was the danger she hadn't planned to face.

CHAPTER THIRTEEN

Tessa woke early on Saturday morning, already smiling. She had a plan, a surprise for Jet, and it was years since she'd been excited about something like this. Staying in bed simply wasn't an option.

She and Jet had been meeting up pretty much every day, and Tessa had stopped trying to fight the feelings creeping up on her. It was on Thursday that she'd realised. She'd gone down to the seafront with a packet of biscuits after work, and they'd sat on the path in front of Jet's beach hut, their feet dangling over the sand, watching the sunset and the stars appear one by one. She'd watched the lights reflect off Jet's eyes as she'd stared out over the sea, and she'd realised that she wanted more of her.

She wanted more evenings dodging around each other in the kitchen, making dinner and talking. She wanted more opportunities to tell Jet about the latest research in sustainable packaging and how she was going to convince local companies to use it. She wanted to talk to her about mer technology and how they used the movement of the tides and currents as their main source of energy, storing it using springs made from some polymer that Tessa had never heard of.

Sometimes, she would walk back from the beach in the dark, long after she'd usually be in bed on a work night, and the euphoria of seeing Jet would fade for a moment. What was she doing? Was she buying into all this mermaid shit, actually believing such an impossible thing? The sky seemed to darken in those moments, and she found herself hunching a little, her arms wrapped around herself. The voice in her head sounded like Hannah's.

Sometimes, just sometimes, she heard herself answering back to the Hannah-voice. Asking why it mattered. So what if she was buying in to it? What was so wrong with believing in magic and wonderful things, trying to reach back through the years to the innocence of childhood, when mermaids had just been a fact of life.

She wanted it to be real so badly. She wanted to see Jet swim with a tail, watch her transform. She wanted to sit by the sea with her, sit closer, link arms as they walked. She wanted to lean into her and kiss her.

She tried not to give those thoughts too much time. Most of all, she wanted to help Jet find peace, and that might mean helping her to leave Whitby. Leave Tessa.

Tessa had always wanted more than people could give her, and that was okay. She'd learned to accept it and move on. Her therapist back in her twenties, when she'd actually made time to *go* to one of those, had told her that all thoughts were allowed; it was acting on those thoughts that had to be controlled.

Tessa was damn good at control.

But today was going to be something different. Something fun. She made herself linger over breakfast and not run straight down to the beach. She had a stop to make first, and she couldn't get there too early.

It was nearly eleven a.m. when she walked down the beach toward Jet, who was sitting out front of her beach hut.

"Morning," Jet called. "I was just thinking of walking up to yours."

"Well, I'm glad you didn't," Tessa said, shading her eyes as she looked up. "How would you like to go surfing with me instead?"

Jet's eyebrows shot up, and she tilted her head. "Surfing?" She glanced out to sea. The tide was perfect for it. Tessa had checked the local tide tables. The weather was cooperating too, with a healthy wind whipping up the waves, and only a few high clouds scudding past. There was a group of teenagers already out on their boards.

"I know it's probably not something you've done, but I wanted you to have a good time out on the sea. It's been disappointing for you, hasn't it, the last week or two?" God, only two weeks. That was all the time she'd known Jet. It felt like a hundred times that much.

Tessa felt self-conscious, then. What did she know about Jet and what she wanted? Maybe she hated the idea of being even closer to her home and yet so far away. She shrugged and looked away, not wanting to see Jet's displeasure. "I thought it might be good for you to have fun in the sea. The human way. You don't have to, though, it's—"

"That would be amazing," Jet said, her smile audible in her voice. When Tessa turned to check that she wasn't imagining it, Jet was already standing, practically vibrating with excitement, and Tessa found herself grinning as hard as she ever had. "I've been watching them out there every day, and it looks brilliant. I'd love to have a go. Thanks, Tessa."

Tessa stumbled over a response, tugging on her hair, but thankfully, Jet was running back into her beach hut. Then, reappearing. "I don't have a swimsuit," she said.

"Oh." Tessa bit her lip. "I guess wear your underwear under the wetsuit?" She held out her own wetsuit to demonstrate.

She was definitely not thinking about Jet naked under her wetsuit.

"Ooo." Jet jumped down and came over to finger the material. "This is fascinating stuff. I was wondering what these felt like. I didn't expect them to be this thick. Or stretchy. Wait, there's only one. Aren't you going in?"

"Just try to stop me. This is my own, but the boards and your wetsuit are back at the hire place. They'll want to check your height before they decide which board to give you and get you to sign a waiver."

Tessa knew the guys at the rental well. Dan and Ellie were in their fifties, at least, and had seen her surfing since she and Gabe were kids. When Gabe had become obsessed with rugby league, Tessa had carried on surfing. It was one of the few things from her later childhood that wasn't tainted by thoughts of him. Dan and Ellie already knew Tessa-without-Gabe. They'd never looked to the side of her as if she'd lost a limb.

Dan took them down to the waterline to take Jet through the basics, then nodded over to Tessa. "You all right to take it from here, Tess? Don't go far out on her first go, you know the drill."

Tessa nodded. "Thanks, Dan, I've got it." She pushed her hair out of her eyes. "You ready, Jet?"

"Let's do it."

She led Jet out into the water, showing her when to lie on the board to start paddling. Jet was unsurprisingly relaxed about the cold of the water, and with the wind and tide in the right conditions, it wasn't long before they were able to try catching some waves.

She concentrated on helping Jet rather than surfing for herself, giving Jet timing hints. To start with, she left her own board back on the beach to bob shoulder-deep in the water and hold Jet's board steady.

Jet was not very good. At first, Tessa was worried that it would frustrate her the way it had Tessa when she'd first started out. She and Gabe had sulked terribly after a long day of not enough waves and then, doing badly with the few they could catch. But Jet seemed to love it. Every time she fell off, she came up laughing her head off, gulping water once or twice, and laughing even harder about that. Tessa couldn't help laughing with her, catching her by the biceps if she went down close enough, their faces bowing toward each other, creased up with giggles.

Jet tipped her head back, brushing her hair out of her eyes and making a face as it stuck to her fingers. "Ugh, my thighs are killing me. Give me a break, yeah? Fetch your board and show me what you've got instead."

They paddled out to the waves again, sitting astride the boards for a bit and letting a few peaks ride underneath them. Tessa sat with her hands on her thighs, watching the pattern of the waves and picking out the best place to rise.

"Okay, I'm going in. You all right without me?"

Jet waved a hand. "Don't worry, I can swim."

Tessa shook her head fondly and didn't bother going off on her usual rant about confidence being no substitute for the buddy system. She wouldn't be far anyway.

She dropped into a paddling position, pulling herself through the water. As always, the world seemed to distill down. The usual concerns and issues of the day, of being *Tessa*, disappeared, and she was nothing but muscle and joints, breath and awareness of the water, the wind, the location of the other surfers, and the rhythm of the waves themselves.

As the sea rose up into a perfect, smooth ridge, she looked to the right, picked out her path. She gave herself one last push, then put her hands on the board and hopped up, one leg ahead and one behind, into a deep lunge.

She knew the moment she got a good line, the euphoria rising in her lungs like the wave itself. A little bend here, a press of her toe there, and she was rising up the front of the wave. Just a bit farther, just a bit more, ducking down, and the tube appeared.

The wave curled over her head. The surf wasn't too big that morning, but with her head tucked low and her back knee right down on the board, Tessa was able to drift through that perfect blue tunnel, reaching out to brush the water as it rose to her left. It felt timeless, limitless, the best kind of rush.

A little wobble, a little wrong turn, and she felt her balance going. She threw herself off backward and let the water tumble her head over heels, bumping off the sand in the shallows. She finally broke the surface and punched the air with a whoop before swimming to her board.

"That was amazing," Jet yelled. "Freaking awesome, how do you do that?" She tried to shuffle down and paddle over but tipped off the board and fell in, laughing.

Tessa grinned and paddled out to her instead. "Want to try again?"

Jet spat a perfect stream of seawater at her and wriggled back onto her board. "Only if you don't expect me to do what you did."

"I've been surfing since I was a kid. This is your first try."

"It looked extremely cool."

Tessa smiled and looked away. She couldn't imagine herself looking cool, but if she wanted anyone to think of her that way, it would be Jet.

❖

They made a few more runs before their rental time ran out. Jet managed to get up on her feet once or twice, even riding a wave for a short time before tumbling into the water. By the time they carried their boards up to Dan and Ellie, Jet's cheeks were flushed, and her eyes sparkled. She'd never looked more beautiful.

"Do you want to walk up to mine for a bit?" Tessa asked, suddenly awkward, as if she was asking for a date or something. Ridiculous. Jet had stayed the night plenty of times already. It wasn't anything special. "I mean, I know you haven't got a shower in your beach hut, and I thought…well, it's uncomfortable to be salty and sticky."

"That would be amazing," Jet said, and Tessa's breathing settled back to normal. Jet tugged at her own hair. "I don't know how you humans manage with your hair. How do you stop it getting like *this*?" She held up a massive tangle.

Tessa tried not to look too horrified. "Uh, wow, that looks hard to brush."

"Brush?"

They both stopped and looked at each other. Jet was the first to break. "I have no idea what you mean by brush," she admitted.

"You don't *brush your hair*?" Tessa was trying very hard, but she could hear the incredulity in her own voice. "Comb it?"

Jet's face fell. "It's *different* now. Human hair isn't sensory. For us, it spreads out in the water, each strand can move independently, and it can sense vibrations. We don't need to do anything to it to stop it getting tangled. It would be like your fingers getting tangled."

Tessa was aware she was staring and clicked her jaw shut. "Right. Okay. Uh, do you want me to brush it for you?"

"Would you?"

Her cheeks were heating, but she nodded. "Yeah, of course." She cleared her throat so her voice wasn't quite as squeaky. "Sure."

"Thank you, it's been doing my head in."

"No problem." They walked on a little. "What did you think of surfing?"

Jet grinned so hard, her eyes almost disappeared behind her cheeks. "It was brilliant. So incredibly human. I never would have thought of an activity on the ocean to be un-mer, but it was completely different to anything I've ever done."

"How so?"

She hummed in thought, tipping her head to watch the clouds scud across the sky. "Gravity and balance are important to you guys, and surfing is all about that, isn't it? I'm used to being surrounded by water and having a lot more power in my tail, of course. Though at the same time, I could see the way you moved being a lot more familiar. Those tiny movements you made on the board making much larger, smooth turns. Maybe I'd notice more familiarity if I were a bit better at it."

"I wonder what you'd think of it if you got a chance to go scuba diving. I've only done it once, but it felt like flying to me."

Jet nodded. "Yes, that's a good way to describe it, I guess. Flying underwater."

"Like a penguin." Tessa nudged her with her shoulder. "No wonder you're a bit clumsy on land."

"Hey!"

By the time they reached Tessa's house, she was smiling so much, her cheeks hurt. "You go ahead and have a shower," she said. "I'll put the laundry on. Oh, use plenty of conditioner."

"Right," said Jet slowly. "Conditioner."

She laughed. "It's on the side, next to the shampoo."

Jet nodded, pulling her lips between her teeth and looking altogether lost. Tessa hesitated. "You want me to show you?"

"Would you?"

There was something warming and precious about being trusted like this. "Sure," Tessa said and tried not to show how much it was swelling inside her chest, bigger than it should be, surely. She led Jet upstairs and held out the two bottles. "Use this first," she said, shaking the shampoo bottle. "Get your hair wet, scrub it in, then rinse it out. Uh, don't let it get in your eyes. When it's all out, put loads of this one in, then rinse it out too. It'll feel slimy, but don't worry if you can't get it all out. It'll help me brush it."

"Thanks, Tessa," she said.

Tessa fought the urge to curl up around the gratitude and hold it tight to her chest and instead mumbled something hopeless and escaped.

Get ahold of yourself, she thought firmly. These feelings were amplified out of control, and that couldn't be fair to either of them. She was helping a friend, she told herself. There was nothing more to it.

Jet came downstairs as Tessa was putting away the dry crockery from breakfast, the washer-dryer rumbling in the corner. Jet was wearing a clean set of her own clothes this time, and Tessa had to squash the disappointment that sneaked in. She rushed through her own shower, toweling her short hair dry before picking up a handful of products, combs, and brushes and finding Jet in the kitchen.

"I made you some tea," Jet said. "Now, where do you want me?"

"Anywhere," she replied, and must have gone flame red when she heard how painfully sincere she sounded. "Uh, living room?"

She settled Jet on a cushion on the floor and sat behind her on the sofa, draping a towel over Jet's shoulders and under her hair. "How's it looking, Doctor?" Jet teased.

Tessa nudged her, relieved that she was joking, oblivious to Tessa's tension. "It'll be fine," she said, though it looked a total mess. "I'll put some of this oil in it to help. It'll take a little while, but I'll try not to tug too bad."

For a while, there was silence as they both concentrated, Tessa on her job and Jet on probably not reacting to the tugs on various knots. "Where did you learn to do this?" Jet asked. "Your hair's short so it can't get that knotty, surely?"

"You'd be surprised. But I used to have long hair. And…I used to do my mum's hair all the time."

"Oh? Do you not anymore?"

Tessa paused, fingers still sunk into Jet's hair. "She died when I was twelve."

Jet gasped, a small, soft sound, and put a hand up to Tessa's knee. "I'm sorry. That must have been awful."

Tessa swallowed hard and forced her hands to move. "It was. There was a train crash coming back from one of my brother's rugby matches."

Jet turned, tugging her hair out of Tessa's hands, leaving her with nothing to shield herself. "Your brother?"

Tessa nodded. "My twin. He died too." She tried to smile through a shaking breath. "Not me, though. Not a scratch on me."

Jet was kneeling in front of her now, hands resting on Tessa's knees. She didn't say anything, just looked at her. Invited her to feel. Tessa wanted to tell her not to do that, or she'd be drowned by the wave of it. Tessa had always been too much. Too much and never enough.

"He was the only boy, you know?" she said, barely above a whisper. "I think it destroyed my dad. I think that's what took him away from us." She held Jet's gaze, searching, waiting for Jet to stop her, shut the floodgates while she still could, but Jet never did, her fingers stroking, scratching against Tessa's jeans-clad knees.

"I can't tell the others," she said, almost blurted. These thoughts she'd built herself around, secret and painful as a pearl. "It would hurt them too much. Hannah, she was the eldest, so she had to take over from Mum. She made us do homework and packed our lunch in the mornings. Joanie was only little. I think it hit her the worst, losing Mum. Losing Gabe hit Dad worst, and losing Mum hit Joanie. She was a tearaway."

Jet wiped the tears from Tessa's cheek. She hadn't even realised they were falling. "And what about you?" she asked.

"What about me?"

"You tell me all about how it impacted the others, but what about you?"

Tessa stared, and now the words wouldn't come, trapped inside in a whirlwind of chaos and confusion, so many of them that they couldn't all get out at once, so none could. Jet cupped her cheeks, looked into her soul, and pulled her close as she cried.

CHAPTER FOURTEEN

Jet crawled up onto the sofa without breaking the hug. Tessa clung to her, crying softly, and Jet stroked her hair. She wanted to surround Tessa in safety, show her that she didn't have to be strong and hold this in all the time, pretending she was okay. Her chest ached with the sorrow of it. She hated the idea of Tessa feeling like she had to put her fears and hurts aside for others all the time. She was such a kind, caring person. Jet wanted to protect her, give some of that back.

She had to admit that she'd felt like this for a while. Maybe even since the first night, when a drunk Tessa had been so apologetic for not believing in mermaids anymore but had instinctively tried to build Jet up and encourage her. Jet shifted her face, pressing her nose to Tessa's still-damp hair, and closed her eyes.

What was she doing? She was supposed to be trying to get home, not trying to find a way to get closer to a human woman, relishing every moment she had near her. Having Tessa in her arms made her feel like there had been something missing her whole life, and she'd found it, but it *couldn't* be. She couldn't be thinking this way.

Tessa pulled back and wiped her eyes on her sleeve. "I'm sorry," she said, lifting both feet onto the sofa so her knees shielded her from the world. She looked small curled up like that, and Jet wanted to wrap her up again. Say something stupid like, *I'll protect you now. You can let go.*

"You don't have anything to be sorry about," she said instead.

"At least we sorted your hair out. I hope it didn't pull too badly."

Jet shook her head and ran her fingers through her hair, pulling it over one shoulder. "Thank you for that, it was driving me mad."

Tessa's eyes followed her fingers as they combed through her hair. "It looks much better now." She blushed. "Not that it wasn't beautiful before, of course."

Jet paused and regarded Tessa. "You think it looks beautiful?" What was she doing? Why was she taking this risk? She could fuck it all up, and for what?

Tessa inhaled, a little gasp. "I…uh…well…"

She should laugh it off. She should leave this woman behind and concentrate on getting home.

This kind, beautiful, thoughtful woman.

Jet said nothing. It felt like taking her armour off, then patrolling, like hunting in the deeps. It felt like getting caught up in a humpback whale's bubble ring, vast and terrifying, and at the same time, a type of magic.

Tessa gripped the material of her jeans over her knees. "I think all of you is beautiful," she said on a breath, her voice soft but steady. She looked like she was facing a battle of her own, chin up.

Jet should have thanked her and left. Instead, she brushed one finger over the back of Tessa's hand, sending a shiver through Tessa, goose bumps forming on her arm where the shirt had been pushed up a little.

Tessa shifted, her knees falling toward Jet, and her hand turning so that their fingertips just touched. "Tell me I'm misreading this," she said, that voice that sent prickles of desire up Jet's spine. "Tell me you don't want this."

Jet said nothing. She dived into the deeps instead. She pulled Tessa in by her wrist, her other hand coming up to thread into Tessa's short hair, and kissed her.

Tessa fell toward her with a squeak that turned into a moan as their lips collided. She caught herself on the arm of the sofa behind Jet and kissed back, her lips opening under Jet's, soft and warm and like life itself. Jet had never kissed as a human, but she couldn't pretend that was the reason for the way her entire body, every nerve, became perfectly attuned and alert to Tessa. She felt every shift of her neck, every shuddering breath.

Tessa moved closer, and Jet realised she'd been pulling her; the hand that wasn't buried in Tessa's hair was now sliding under her shirt and wrapping around a warm, slim waist. Tessa moved to straddle her, tipping Jet's head back to kiss her more, deeper.

Should could take a hike. Jet wasn't leaving now, or any time tonight, if she had anything to say about it. The time for *should* had passed the moment Jet had felt those perfect lips on her own. Maybe it had always been inevitable. Now all that was left was doing everything in her power to get closer, to inhabit Tessa the way Tessa was beginning to inhabit her, crawling under her skin and living in her mind, every tilt of her sharp face, every glint of the sun off her hair. Jet had never surrendered to anyone in her life, but she surrendered to Tessa.

❖

There was a sharp, jarring noise shrieking at Jet, dragging her out of her dreams and gasping into wakefulness to stare around for the threat in the dark. Beside her, Tessa grumbled, and Jet threw out a hand to shield her until she knew what that infernal noise was.

Tessa reached out to the bedside table and picked up her phone, blinding both of them for a moment but stopping the noise. "Hello?" Her voice was rough and smoky with sleep.

Maybe some of that roughness was Jet's fault, too. She lay back beside Tessa and pretended she didn't feel smug.

"Is that Tessa Bordeaux?" asked the tinny voice from the other end of the phone call.

"Speaking."

"This is Amy from Beechwood Care Home. It's about your dad, Tom?"

Jet felt Tessa tense under her roving fingers and sat up next to her, alert.

"It's nothing serious," Amy said, though judging from how Tessa's fingers clenched into the duvet, it wasn't working. "He's had a bit of a fall, and we've taken him to hospital to be on the safe side."

"The one in Whitby?" Tessa asked, her voice strangled.

"Yes. I'm sorry to call you so early, but I thought you and your sisters would want to know sooner rather than later."

"Yes, of course. Can we come and visit now?"

"Let me check with reception," she said, and the phone crackled as if she'd taken it away from her ear. Voices sounded in the distance, inaudible, and Tessa remained tense, sitting ramrod straight. Jet rubbed her thumb along her spine and wished she could do something.

"Hello, Tessa? Yes, they say you're welcome to come in and wait. They might be able to let you in to see him, but you might be better off waiting until visiting hours—"

"I'll be right there," Tessa said, flipping the duvet off her legs and scrambling out of bed. "Have you contacted my sisters yet?"

"I've got hold of Joan, and I'm about to call Hannah now."

"Okay, thank you. I'll see you there." She hung up and flicked the lamp on, grabbing at some clothes. Jet could see the tension ramping up in every movement, and she was beginning to mutter to herself. Jet glanced around and spotted a set of drawers, half-open, and tugged a shirt out of it. "Here, Tessa."

Tessa stood and looked at Jet like she'd forgotten she was there. "Thanks." She twisted the T-shirt in her hands, looking lost, and Jet's heart clenched.

She stepped closer and squeezed Tessa's biceps gently, rubbing her thumbs across the bare skin. "You get dressed, okay? I'll make you a cup of tea."

Tessa's lip wobbled slightly. Then she nodded. Jet put her own clothes on quickly and went downstairs to make tea. The mugs from last night were still in the living room. She stood at the doorway a moment and looked at the sofa as if she could see the imprint of the two of them sitting side by side. Of Tessa astride her. Of her world tilting.

She looked away, forced herself to get on with the task at hand.

Tessa was muttering to herself when she walked into the kitchen. Jet caught her and gave her the tea. "Stay still a moment. Just drink and tell me what you need."

She slumped. "I don't know," she said, her voice small.

"Bag?"

She nodded. "Phone, too. And…" She glanced up at Jet a moment, then back at her tea.

"What?"

She could almost see the argument going on in Tessa's mind and could do nothing about it. At last, Tessa glanced up again, those big brown eyes guarded but hopeful. "Do you mind coming with me?" And then, hurriedly, "You don't have to, it's fine if not."

"Of course I'll come." Without thinking, she kissed Tessa's head in the pale dawn light.

It felt like another tipping point as she leaned back. Like last night wasn't a one-time thing. Sex could be brushed off, almost, but kisses and emotional support and brushing a strand of blond hair behind her ear, all those things were harder to deny. Harder to walk away from.

"Thanks," said Tessa, smiling crookedly up at her.

Jet didn't think walking away was an option.

❖

The sun was rising as Jet stood at the roadside, waiting for Tessa to lock her door. She stayed quiet as they walked through the sleeping town. Tessa was very obviously wound tight, the fingers of her left hand tapping a frantic rhythm on her thigh as she glared at the pavement ahead.

Jet found herself mentally clawing for solid ground. Now that there was nothing concrete to do to help Tessa, she felt discombobulated, thrown off. Things had been clear in her mind before she'd allowed herself to fall toward Tessa. Before, she'd been able to hold herself separate. She could tell herself that Tessa was nothing more than a distraction, a pretty woman, a friend, perhaps. Her mission to get back home was unaffected by her. Now, however…

Kissing her, falling into bed with her, had felt like a door slamming shut. Worse than that, it made her think that the door had been closing behind her for some time, that it wasn't all on Tessa.

What if she never got home?

Tessa crossed the road and led them through a wooded park. Jet looked up and stopped, smiling as a flurry of wind knocked some autumn leaves off the trees they were passing, showering her with them.

Tessa turned, her hands in the pocket of her long black coat, and smiled. It was small but genuine. "What's up?"

"Sorry," Jet said, starting to walk again but holding her hand out as more leaves started to fall. "I've never seen autumn on land before. It's beautiful."

Tessa tipped her head back and watched light yellow leaves drift across the dawn sky. "It is, isn't it?"

Jet considered, then tucked her arm in Tessa's, leading her onward. Tessa glanced at her, and Jet feigned nonchalance. This was a perfectly normal thing to do and didn't matter at all. Tessa's cheeks pinked, and she looked down, but now as she walked, she smiled slightly, and her fingers no longer tapped.

Chapter Fifteen

Tessa drew strength from Jet's arm linked with hers as they walked up to the hospital. Logically, she knew Dad was fine; he'd just had a fall. That was common in dementia cases, and he'd been early onset. It shouldn't be surprising that it was progressing to this point.

Telling herself didn't seem to help, though. Hospitals would never be somewhere she was comfortable, not after the train. Not after stitches on her forehead from a nurse while somewhere else, doctors had huddled around her mum and brother, trying to revive them.

She assumed they'd tried. Nobody had ever told her. She'd been twelve, after all, and had been nobody's priority right then. People didn't tell twelve-year-olds things like that, certainly not in the nineties.

She found the entrance to the hospital and let Jet's hand slip from hers as she approached the receptionist. "I'm here to see Tom Bordeaux. Someone said I might be able to see him out of visiting hours if he wasn't in with the doctors."

The receptionist clicked away at a computer. "Take a seat, love. The doctor will come out in a minute, I'm sure."

"Tessa Bordeaux?" Tessa turned to see a small woman with a sensible bun and sensible shoes and a reassuring smile on her face. "I'm Amy, we spoke on the phone."

Tessa took her hand. "Yes, of course, thank you. Is there any news?" She was aware of Jet approaching, standing beside her and a half step behind.

"He's been for X-rays, and there's no injury to his head. That's always our first priority, though he said he didn't think he'd bumped it on the way down. They think he might have a fracture in his ankle, but the film wasn't quite clear. They've taken him in to have another look."

Tessa let out a long breath, enough tension leaving her shoulders that a headache started to recede. She hadn't even noticed herself getting one. "How is he in himself?"

Amy looked amused. "Very unimpressed with having to stay still. He does say he's not in much pain, says it's all a lot of fuss over nothing, but…" She shrugged. "Better to be safe than sorry."

"Definitely. Can I see him, do you think?"

"As far as I know. He went for another X-ray about ten minutes ago, so he shouldn't be long. Why don't you take a seat?"

Tessa sagged, grateful for Jet's arm tucking into hers again. "C'mon," Jet said, tugging her over to the white plastic seats. "How are you doing?"

"Relieved," she said. "Sorry I dragged you along."

"Don't be daft." Jet held her gaze. "I'm happy to help if I can. You're allowed to ask for help, you know?"

She laughed softly and looked away, unable to stand the sincerity in her eyes. "One of my colleagues said something similar recently. Must be the universe's way of telling me that my human-disaster side is showing."

"Or maybe it's the universe's way of telling you that you deserve support," Jet said dryly.

She snorted, making a little *psh* sound. "As Sophie would say, sounds fake but okay."

"Ms. Bordeaux?" Amy reappeared in the reception area. "Your dad's back, if you'd like to come see him now."

Tessa stood, following Amy so quickly that she didn't notice that Jet was right beside her. She didn't know how she felt about that, but Amy was pulling another chair over to put beside Dad's bed and tugging the curtains around them.

Tessa took a seat rather than deal with it. She swallowed and tried not to notice the way the industrial-looking bed frame made her father look so small. Against the crisp white sheets, his skin looked sallow and wrinkled, like old parchment, and it struck her how fucking unfair it all was, how young he was in the scheme of things. She forced it down, swallowed it and tucked the anger and grief away where it always lived. "Hey, Dad."

"Ey up, love," he said, sounding drained. "What a load of fuss over nothing, hey?"

"It's not nothing, Dad, they say you might have a fracture."

"Rubbish, I feel fine. Why won't they let me go home? I'm missing *Death in Paradise*."

She checked her watch. "No, it's still only seven in the morning, you'll be fine."

He shook his head. "I just this minute had it on. That young ginger man, what's his name? He was about to reveal the killer." He let his head flop back on the pillow with a petulant huff, and Tessa smiled fondly.

"I'll help you set it up on iPlayer when we get back."

But Dad had turned his attention toward Jet. "Ah, Harriet, love, I haven't seen you in ages. How's the pub business treating you?"

Jet blinked and tilted her head, no doubt oblivious to Tessa's sudden spike of panic because in all this time, she'd forgotten to tell her anything about Dad's situation. "I'm sorry, you must have me mixed up with someone else. I'm Jet."

She held out her hand, and Dad took it with a little "Oh." He rubbed his forehead with the fingers of his other hand. "Sorry about that. Must be getting old. What did you say your name was?"

"Jet," she repeated, leaning closer. "I'm Tessa's"—*oh fuck*—"friend."

"Tessa?" he said, his forehead crinkling. His fingers were starting to tap, a nervous tick she recognised in herself.

Tessa squashed the pang of grief she could never train herself out of and tugged Jet to her feet. "Excuse us a minute," she said, putting on her best professional smile.

"Of course, take your time," he said. Tessa wondered bitterly who he thought she was. If he knew she was his daughter but had forgotten her name, or if in his own mind, he was forty years younger and not even considering having children.

She still had her hand around Jet's wrist as they burst back into the waiting room. She dropped it as she realised how tightly she must have been gripping and hoped she hadn't hurt her. "Sorry," she said, clearing her throat. "I should've told you. My dad's got dementia."

Jet tilted her head. "I don't know what that is."

"Yeah," she said, exhausted. "I don't know what it is exactly, either. It happens to some people when they get old, or in the case of my dad, when he was about forty-five. He started forgetting things and getting mood swings, and of course, the forgetting made him anxious. My older sister Hannah looked after him for a long time, but it got to the point where he would forget he lived with her and try to go to his old house in the middle of the night or walk out the front door and…well, we had to put him in assisted living after the police found him sitting on a riverbank half-frozen last January."

"That's awful," Jet said, taking Tessa's hand. She realised she'd been tapping her fingers on the wall behind her and bit down the urge to clench her fists, not with Jet's calloused hand holding her this gently. She had a flash of a memory from years ago, when Mum had still been around. A little bird had flown into the house, and Mum had caught it, cradled it in her palms as its chest heaved with panic. She felt like that now, Jet's hands warm and strong around her fluttering heartbeat, holding her patiently until she could get ahold of herself.

The reception door opened and Tessa jumped, startled, as Hannah bustled in with her usual level of noise. "Don't touch anything, Benjamin, and keep quiet. Remember, a hospital is a place for people to get better. They don't want boys running around causing havoc and getting underfoot. Now, go sit over there while I talk to the receptionist and—"

"Jet! Look, Mum, Jet's here with Tessa, I told you about her, didn't I? She's a mermaid." Ben ran over, ignoring Hannah's pursed lips and air of displeasure. He bounced in front of Jet as Tessa whipped her hand away and put it behind her back as if hiding a treat.

"Hi, Ben," Jet said, grinning.

Hannah vacillated between bossing the receptionist around and reprimanding everyone in sight and finally marched up to Tessa, her sensible heels clicking sharply. "Morning, Tessa, I didn't know you were coming in."

Tessa shrugged. "I didn't know you were, I suppose."

"Of course I was, what do you take me for? My father's in hospital."

"Isn't he Tessa's father too?" Jet said, frowning.

Hannah blinked, open-mouthed, as if she'd never been corrected in her life. Tessa couldn't remember if she ever had.

Ben tugged at Jet's hand. "Jet, come show me more fighting."

"No," Hannah snapped. "Ben, go sit down and play on your Switch."

"Okay. Jet, come see my new game."

Jet sent Tessa an amused look and pretended to be unable to resist Ben's strength, trailing after him to the plastic seats.

Tessa realised too late that she was smiling like a sap. Hannah rounded on her, and she wiped the smile off. "I cannot believe you," Hannah whisper-yelled. "Why on earth did you bring her *here*? Are you trying to give Dad a heart attack?"

"What? No, of course not."

"And I don't know what the whole *mermaid* thing is. I swear, Tessa, if you've taught my son some sort of lesbian slang word—"

Tessa couldn't help but burst out laughing. "God's sake, Hannah, don't be ridiculous."

"I don't find this a laughing matter," she said, crossing her arms. "You know this would break Dad's heart if he found out. I can't believe you would do this right when he's so vulnerable."

She was walking with me, Tessa wanted to say, but she could feel the exhaustion, the little voice in the back of her mind asking, *what's the point*? It wasn't like she ever listened.

"...barely spent any time with him at all last Sunday before rushing off, and it's not as if you'll take a day off work to go see him. I suppose it's lucky he had this fall on a weekend because I imagine if he'd had an accident while you were at work, he'd still be lying there, bleeding out. And then you have the audacity to—"

Tessa could feel herself drifting off into some dark corner of her mind as she always did when Hannah got a bee in her bonnet about something. She'd float away on a sea of not caring, Hannah would work out all her frustrations, all muted and only just audible, and they'd move on. Of course, all the words came back to bite Tessa at night, when she was trying to sleep, but at least they didn't hit her right now, in public, when anyone could see her crying.

She didn't notice Jet walk up behind Hannah at first until she leaned in, her face close to Hannah's ear. "Say one more word, human, and I'll show you an accident."

Hannah squeaked and jumped, turning to Jet with wide eyes, stuttering something. Jet glared at her, the lips that had been plush and soft under Tessa's last night were thin and hard, and her eyes flashed with anger.

"Are you threatening me?" Hannah tried to draw herself up and face off against Jet.

Jet smiled in a slightly disturbing and disturbingly attractive way. "Yes."

"I…well, I never," Hannah said because she always had modeled herself on a Karen from the fifties, and what was happening? Tessa hadn't allowed herself these kinds of thoughts in years. Hannah turned her shocked offense on Tessa. "Are you going to let her talk to me like this?"

Tessa shook her head, not to agree, but because she did not have the emotional energy to deal with this. She wanted to be curled up in Jet's arms again; she wanted it to be the night before; she wanted to be laughing in the surf, anywhere but here. "Forget it, we're leaving," she said.

"Tessa, your *father* is here in hospital, and you're choosing her?"

Jet put her arm through Tessa's as they turned toward the door. "Oh, now he's her father, is he?"

"I do not believe you. Tessa, come *back* here. We are your *family*."

Tessa tried to find that distance again, push Hannah's voice to the back of her mind where her words could be saved for later, but Jet's arm was too grounding. She swallowed hard and held on to her tears to smile at Ben, who was looking up at them with big eyes. "See you in a bit, kiddo," she said, ruffling his hair.

"Is she mad because of me?" he asked quietly.

"No," Jet said firmly. "She's mad because she's got a stick up her arse."

"Jet!" Tessa couldn't help but laugh even as she gaped at her. Ben slapped his hand over his mouth, his eyes crinkling up.

"Come on, let's get you out of here," Jet said, casting another vicious glare at Hannah, who was *still* talking. Somehow, the words didn't seem to be cutting as deep.

Walking out into the cold autumn air felt like surfacing, and Tessa took a moment to breathe. Then she turned to Jet, eyebrows raised. "I'll show you an accident? Really?"

Jet groaned and covered her face with both hands. "I don't know, it just came out."

"What does that even mean?" She was laughing now, humour bubbling up through the emotional fog she'd put herself in. Unfortunately, the hurt she'd pushed down saw its chance, and she couldn't stop the giggles from turning into a gulping sob.

"Oh, Tess, come here," Jet said, stopping her and wrapping her up in her arms. Jet was a little shorter, but with Tessa's head bowed low on her shoulder, Jet seemed bigger. All-encompassing.

Tessa was so *tired*. Of trying to hide all the time, of controlling her emotions and being strong and mature when all she wanted to do was scream and call her sisters names.

"Why was your sister blaming you for your dad's fall?"

Tessa sighed. "She wasn't really. She does that when she's upset. Everything's a catastrophe, everything's much more of a problem than other people think, and we're all just one step away from disaster."

"But none of what she was saying made sense. She was ranting about your job, but you weren't at work all day yesterday."

She was pretty sure Jet hadn't overheard Hannah's whole, "Dad will have an instant heart attack and die if he finds out you're gay" thing, which was a relief. "Most of what Hannah says doesn't really make sense. It's her venting."

"Well, it's not fair. You're not her emotional punching bag."

"Leave it," Tessa said, leaning back from the hug to look Jet in the eye. "It's complicated, okay?"

Jet looked resigned. "Okay. Sorry."

She turned to walk again but in a fit of daring, tucked her hand into Jet's. Jet's fingers intertwined with hers, and it felt like walking below a neon sign, *happiness here*. The people walking by, though, didn't seem to notice.

"Hannah's been like that pretty much since Mum and Gabe died," Tessa said into the silence. It was strange. She didn't feel like she had to explain, more like it was okay if she wanted to, and she trusted Jet. Maybe more than she should. She'd only known her a few weeks, after all. "She's the oldest, so she took over the job of mothering us, and I think she never quite figured out how to do it without overdoing it, you know?"

Jet shrugged slightly but squeezed her hand in encouragement.

"Full disclosure," Tessa admitted. "But I think all of us took on these particular roles. My little sister is the rebel. It's like she actually works at being the black sheep of the family. And me…I don't know. Sometimes, I think I tried to be the boy of the family once Gabe died."

Jet didn't say anything, just held her hand and looked at her with a compassion that Tessa couldn't take head-on. She rubbed her temple, wishing she could pull the tears that were threatening to fall again back into her head, that there was a switch somewhere on her face so they couldn't embarrass her.

"Thing is," she said with a forced little laugh, "I was always a tomboy. Hannah was always bossy, and Joanie always had the most awful tantrums, way before Mum died, so I don't know. Maybe it's nothing to do with that. Maybe that's just who we are, but I'll never know, will I? I don't know. It kind of bothers me. Joanie says I did too much therapy in my twenties, but recently, I've been thinking maybe I didn't do enough." She looked up at Jet. "God, sorry for off-loading on you like this."

Jet unlinked their fingers to put an arm around Tessa's waist, tugging her close. "Don't be daft. You've had a rough morning, and I'll keep telling you as long as you need to hear it: you're allowed to ask for help."

Tessa nudged her with a hip, which knocked their rhythm off as they walked.

"I think I understand what you mean, though. How much of what we are is what was done to us? Like, am I a warrior because of my dad's injury? Or would I always have been like this no matter what had happened before I was born?"

Tessa considered. "I think you'd always have been a fighter. I can't imagine you any other way. But maybe it would've been more low-key if your life had all been roses."

Jet thought, nodding. "Still think I'd have had a go at your sister either way."

Tessa laughed. "Yeah. Me too."

❖

They walked on, aimless, and found themselves by the waterfront. In silent agreement, they found the steps down to the beach and took their shoes and socks off, dangling them from their fingers as they walked along the cold sand.

Jet held Tessa's hand again as they walked. She was hyper aware of every centimeter in contact with her skin, every movement, every possibility that her palms were sweaty or had sand on them, and was she holding too tight or too loose?

Or were the people walking the other way going to be homophobic?

She didn't notice the shape in the water until Jet stopped, staring out into the waves. "What is it?" she asked, shading her eyes.

Jet didn't answer, squinting, her brow scrunched up. Then she ran, her hand torn from Tessa's, her arms pumping and legs eating up the sand until she threw herself into the water.

Tessa let out a wordless shout and ran after her, shedding her coat as she went. She gasped with the cold as she threw herself into the water, trying to keep her eyes on Jet as she battled the waves. Jet was already what seemed like a mile away, and Tessa felt a flood of panic for the first time at the thought of losing her.

Jet," she screamed and coughed up water, salt burning the lining of her nose as her jeans tugged at her. Without her surfboard, with waterlogged clothes instead of a wetsuit, the ocean felt more like a vast and dangerous creature than freedom and exhilaration. "Jet!"

There was a thump against her side, her body dragged hip-first through the sea, and through the white screaming panic, she thought of *Jaws*, which had terrified her as a kid. The utter powerlessness, the knowledge of the coming painful death.

And then Jet was in front of her, wide, worried eyes darker than the sea, black curls plastered to her face. "Tessa, you're all right, you're okay."

Tessa twisted sharply to see what was holding her if Jet was in front.

A plump woman with large brown eyes, a flat, slit-like nose and a mass of red hair, longer even than Jet's, held Tessa around the waist. "You okay, human?"

Tessa startled, jerking away. "Jesus. Uh. Hi?" She tried a smile, but her polite people skills were somewhat dampened by her unexpected swim.

Something caught her eye, and she looked into the waist-deep water.

"What…is that a tail?"

The…fuck, the *mermaid* looked at Tessa, then at Jet. "Are you vouching for her?"

Jet nodded. "She knows."

Tessa was vaguely aware that her eyes kept widening as she stared at the coppery scales—scales!—that glinted in the sunlight filtering through clouds and cold water. *She knows*, Jet said, but had Tessa really *known* until she saw a human-fish hybrid for herself? She still wasn't convinced she wasn't hallucinating. Perhaps she'd drowned and hadn't noticed.

She shuddered violently, teeth chattering. The woman—mermaid!—glanced at her sharply. "She's getting too cold." She rose out of the water, and as she did so, her tail shifted into two legs, her nose seemed to appear out of her face along with two ears that Tessa hadn't even noticed were missing. The process was more than a little bit unsettling, reminding her of old werewolf films. The tunic changed shape along with her into a mini dress, and she stood in front of Tessa and Jet, who were still sitting in waist-deep freezing water.

"Have you been staying in the beach hut?" she asked, holding out her hands.

Tessa took one, but Jet stood and threw her arms around the mermaid. Human. Whatever.

"Ugh, what are you doing, you dramatic pea-brain?" the mermaid groaned.

"Shut up, Amber, I'm hugging you. Get over it."

Amber met Tessa's gaze and rolled her eyes. "Come on. Your human is going to get hypothermia. She's too skinny. How do you even cope?" She cocked her head at Tessa.

"Uh. Coats?"

"Oh yeah. Them." She picked Tessa's coat off the beach where she'd dropped it and held it out for Tessa, who flung it over her shoulders. It didn't seem to make much difference to the painful, bone-deep cold. It had been so long since she'd been swimming without a wetsuit.

She realised Jet was still standing in the sea, wiping her eyes. "Jet…"

"I thought you were dead," Jet said to Amber.

Amber's expression softened. "I'm fine."

"I hate you."

"You love me."

"Only out of obligation. How are we related again?"

"Eh, second cousins once removed or something."

"Where have you been?" Jet wiped her eyes with the heel of her hand. "Amber, where the fuck have you *been*? I thought you were dead."

"Look, let's go up to the beach hut," Amber said, glancing at Tessa. Tessa tugged the coat tighter around her while trying not to look cold.

Jet's relief was turning to anger; her face contorted into a snarl. "I thought you were dead, and you turn up here like you've been on some fucking holiday. What, was this all to…to teach me a lesson?"

"I was sorting out your mess, Jet," Amber snapped, marching toward Jet and stopping with her face pushed in toward hers. "Did you think of that? You tried to start up another fucking war because you're a glory hound who doesn't have the most basic understanding of diplomacy and doesn't ever *fucking listen*."

"Hey," Tessa said, clearing her throat to try to stop the shivers. "Uh, do you want to come back to mine and talk this through?" In the warmth. Where there was tea.

Amber sighed. "Jet…c'mon."

Jet glanced over at Tessa and finally seemed to realise they were both still wearing soaking wet clothes. She shivered suddenly and violently and nodded. "Yeah," she said softly.

Tessa wanted to hold out her hand, link their fingers again, but with Amber right there and an unknown quantity, she was afraid. She didn't want to cause problems for Jet, either. They seemed to have enough to work through.

She picked her trainers up from where she'd dropped them. "It's this way," she said to Amber and started walking up the beach, trailed awkwardly by two mermaids in human skin.

CHAPTER SIXTEEN

Jet had never had a hot shower in her life before this month, and now she was wrapped in Tessa's towel dressing gown following her second in twenty-four hours. Tessa herself was fully dressed and in the kitchen doing laundry, the tension all but vibrating off her through the walls. But right now, Jet had to prioritise Amber.

"What happened after…"

"After I used up all my magic to teleport you to safety?" Amber said dryly. "I sort of blacked out."

Jet made an aborted move forward, wanting to grab Amber, check she was really there, really well. "How did you get out?"

"Well," she said, her lips pinched, and her words with a viciously sarcastic tone. "Turns out, if you take away the person trying to violently attack everyone, the battle sort of ends."

Jet gaped at her. "I was not trying to…*they* attacked first. I was defending us, against mounting odds, I might say."

"A sixteen-year-old attacked first. A traumatised sixteen-year-old who'd recently lost his parents and who would have been restrained by the leader if you hadn't jumped forward and started shedding blood."

"That's bullshit, Amber, there were three of them and more coming down the rise, all armed to the teeth—"

"For hunting, yeah. You know the Knarr go after bigger prey than us."

Jet shook her head. "I don't know how they got to you, but this is all a bit too fucking convenient. What were they doing settling in the buffer zone if they're so innocent, huh?"

Amber sighed and rubbed her head. "They didn't *get* to me, Jet. I haven't been brainwashed, if that's what you're thinking. The leader, Brede, carried me back to Farn Deeps in surrender."

"So…"

"So your mam's been sorting this all out with me. Marra and I've been healing all the injuries, which, god*damn*, Jet, you caused some gnarly ones. Turns out Knarr don't have many healers or mages."

She slumped and drank her tea, and Jet noticed for the first time how tired she looked, dark circles under her eyes and exhaustion tugging at her limbs. "The last few years have been bad for them. Way worse than for us." She looked at Jet, sorrow heavy in her eyes. "The territory they got in the treaty…the humans have found oil there. They've got those massive rigs up, which, you know, for us, isn't that much of a big deal. But it turns out, some of the Knarr use sonar to hunt."

Jet cocked her head. Tessa appeared in the doorway, leaning against the door frame, her shoulders hunched as if trying to make herself smaller. Jet wanted to reassure her, but this was bigger. This was her whole life, all her people. "What's that got to do with it?" Jet asked.

"Humans use sound waves to survey for oil. I don't really know how, but they send out pulses that screw with the Knarr something awful. Well, actually, just this little group of them. The rest of the clan think they're making it up. Chief Vander has all but kicked the whale hunters out. He calls them malingerers. You know what a paranoid bastard he is."

"Those ones we fought…"

"They're refugees, Jet. The whale hunters. They can't live with the rest of the Knarr, but they don't have anywhere else to go."

There was heavy silence in the room. Jet sat with her hand over her mouth, trying to feel anything other than the guilt that threatened to break her. "Why didn't they say anything? Ask for help before this?"

"The war, obviously. We didn't trust them, and they didn't trust us. Would you have believed it before? Hell, it's not like their own chief believes them."

She closed her eyes and pressed her face into her hands. She felt Tessa's hand on her back and startled before leaning into the touch.

"What now?" Tessa asked.

"There's a summit in three days with the Knarr leaders. We sent a message over to Fiskebank before we got the whole story from Brede, the leader of that little splinter group, and now Vander's got a puffer in his chest about it. You'll need to be there, Jet." She leaned forward and waited until Jet met her gaze. "You need to make a formal apology before we even start to consider next steps."

Jet opened her mouth to argue but deflated. "Yeah." She nodded. "Okay."

Amber raised her eyebrows. "You sure? We can't afford to start the conflict up again, none of us can."

"I'm not going to do that." Jet rolled her eyes. "Look, they could've done things differently too. I didn't throw the first punch, as it were. But I should have listened to you and told Mam when we first found the camp."

"Wow, I should cast you out onto land more often," Amber said wryly.

"Don't you fucking dare."

Amber stood and held out a hand to Tessa. "Well, thank you very much for your hospitality. I appreciate the friendship you've shown my cousin. I never planned to leave her here for this long."

"Of course, no problem," said Tessa, taking her hand.

"I don't think I have to tell you how important it is to us that you keep this a secret, right?" Amber narrowed her eyes. "Because I do know how to enforce your silence by magic."

Tessa gave a sharp laugh. "That won't be necessary."

Amber nodded and smiled brightly, all menace disappearing. "Great. I had a feeling I could trust you." She looked down at Jet. "We should get going."

"Oh, right now?" She had a sudden memory of the surfboard beneath her feet, whipping away from under her, unpredictable. Like she should know what to do, it should be obvious, but it wasn't.

Amber rolled her eyes. "Nah, I thought we'd go on a little road trip and hang out with the Humber clan down south. Yes, now."

Jet stood, looking down at the dressing gown that still smelled of Tessa's perfume. She felt cut adrift.

"I'll get you some clothes," Tessa said, her voice distant.

Amber slapped her own forehead. "That's one of those housecoat things, isn't it? Sorry, if you wouldn't mind, that would be great. Otherwise, I can dry her wet clothes with magic."

"They were Tessa's too," Jet admitted.

"It's no problem," Tessa said, giving that polite smile that was nothing like the crooked, relaxed smile Jet liked so much or the quiet laugh that crinkled her face right up. "Back in a mo."

"I'll come with you." Jet followed Tessa up the stairs and refused to remember last night and tumbling up these same stairs, laughing and tugging on Tessa's hand.

Tessa hunted through her drawers, her back rigid with tension as Jet sat on the bed and stared at her hands. "I've got these track pants here and an old T-shirt. I'm sorry it's not very nice or anything. Do you need a hoodie as well? I think I've got another one here, just a min. Here we go, and here are some socks. Oh, and your shoes are still wet, shit, I don't have any others."

She had her hands pressed up against her eyes when Jet looked up, her shoulders hunched up tight. Jet rose quickly and went to her, rubbing her back. Tessa hunched up further. "It's fine, it's fine," she said, her voice wavering and clearly not fine at all. "I mean, you said you were looking for a way home, it's not like I thought…it's fine. I'm being stupid."

Jet clenched her hands around the clothes, crushing the neat folds. What could she say? She had to go home. That had always been the goal. "I've got to go," she said, and something like anger flared up, anger or grief. "You know I've got to. My people are the most important thing to me, surely you understand that?"

Tessa froze and seemed to shrink further at the same time. "Yes, of course. I understand."

"I mean, we're not the same, are we? I don't even know if we're the same species." She laughed, and it hurt, and that made her even angrier. Of course she would prioritise her people over a human she'd only known a few short weeks. Of course Farn Deeps was more important.

"I know, okay? I know." Tessa turned, her tears wiped away, and her face strangely blank and stiff. Was she no longer upset? That would be…that would be good. It wasn't like Jet wanted her to be upset, but…

Tessa walked past and patted Jet's arm almost dismissively, and she tried not to be hurt by that. "Come on. Your cousin's waiting." She slipped out of the room, and it felt like a metaphor. Jet couldn't do anything but change into Tessa's clothes.

When she came downstairs, Tessa was gone. "She said she had to go into work," Amber said. "I assumed you guys said your good-byes upstairs, but are you okay?"

Jet bit her lip and swallowed hard. "Yeah, I'm fine. Let's go, shall we?"

Amber looked at her, narrowing her eyes in appraisal. "Okay, if you're sure."

"Why wouldn't I be?"

Amber sighed and shook her head. "If you say so, Princess. Turn around, let me tie this amulet on."

Jet lifted up her hair, pulling out the tangles that caught on Amber's fingers as she tied the seal-leather choker around her neck. Her hair was a scrambled mess again. She had a sudden, almost painful wish to have Tessa sitting behind her, untangling it with the comb, her hands gentle, and her knees warm by Jet's shoulders.

She locked the door as they left, slipping Tessa's spare key through the letterbox. She couldn't believe it had only been hours ago that she'd left with Tessa to go to the hospital, tangling their fingers together. She'd been thinking how it would be to stay on land forever. She'd looked up into the autumn leaves, her hand warm in Tessa's, and thought she could handle it. Now it seemed stupid at best, a betrayal of her people at worst.

She tugged her hood up and tucked her hands in the pocket, leading the way toward the beach. She didn't look at the leaves falling around them this time.

When she came to the beach hut, slipping her shoes off and tucking them along with Amber's in one of the boxes lining the wall, she couldn't help but pause at the door, staring out at the sea, the dog walkers marching along the beach in their own little worlds. She thought of sitting there with Tessa, staring out over this same view and talking, sharing their worlds with each other.

"Are you going to get changed back into your tunic?" Amber asked, looking around.

"It got damaged," Jet said, not looking at the bucket full of damp kelp-cloth festering in the corner. "It crackled up in the dry."

"Oh yeah." Amber twisted her lips. "You wouldn't know to keep it wet, I guess."

"The amulet'll work on this, won't it?" Jet fingered the material of Tessa's hoodie.

She considered. "The trousers, no. You'll have to take them off when we get in the water and carry them before you change, but the rest of it should be fine. It won't last long if it's cotton, though. Human fabrics aren't meant to deal with the sea like ours."

Jet tucked her hands into the hoodie pocket and looked down at herself in the grey slouchy fabric, so different to what she'd usually wear. She wondered if she'd still be able to smell Tessa's laundry detergent on the material after she changed or if that would be taken away from her as well as soon as she got everything else back.

She straightened and gathered her armour and spear, pulling the hoodie off to strap them on over the stretchy shirt, a little looser than the one Tessa had given her the first time but still formfitting. The hoodie was big enough to go over the top, hiding them from view even in broad daylight.

"Nice," said Amber, standing back to look at her. "We won't have to wait till nightfall. We can swim out and duck down as soon as there are no humans watching."

Jet nodded and resisted arguing. What would be the point? What did she think was going to happen, that Tessa would run down to the beach and beg her not to go? Even if she did, Jet had to. She couldn't put her own personal happiness in front of the clan. She had to make sure they were all okay.

After all, she could always come back again now that she knew she'd be able to get home. Maybe the amulet would even work on Tessa. Mam had drilled it into her often enough that humans and all the different groups of mer were more related than they thought, that there were too many similarities for there not to be a common ancestor.

She didn't let herself linger on the thought, surely nothing but a stupid pipe dream. Instead, she concentrated on locking up, tucking the key in its hiding place under the eaves, and following Amber down the beach to the waves. They were far out with the low tide, now, and the wind and grey hazy skies meant that the few humans out on the beach were uninterested in the scenery, walking or running for a purpose and not looking toward the water.

Jet had a sudden wave of anxiety as the waves rose to her waist, soaking her human clothes and making her human skin goose bump up with the cold. What if this didn't work? What if she dived under the water, and the amulet rejected her? Had she been on land too long, become too human?

What if Amber didn't notice, or worse, realised she was a lost cause and swam off into the deeps without her? It was irrational, she knew. Amber was not only sensible but idealistic and a powerful mage. She would never leave Jet behind like that, and her amulet wouldn't fail. But still, the thought of never seeing her family again, her clan, was enough to put her heart in her throat.

"You ready?" Amber yelled over the sound of the surf. As a mage, she had no need of an amulet and already had her coppery tail to steady her. They were bobbing in the cold water, already deep enough to reach a human's neck. The waves lifted Jet off the sand beneath her feet. She had a flash of memory, of Tessa frowning at the waves, pushing forward at just the right moment to harness one, standing up on her board, and coasting through beneath the crest as it broke over her head.

Jet looked away from land and tugged the track pants off, catching them and tying them around her waist by the legs. She nodded once to Amber and let herself sink completely, the water meeting itself over her head.

In an instant, she felt the magic flow across her skin, through her bones. The legs she'd almost become used to fused, and she had her tail back, her sensory hair, her gills. God, but she'd missed her gills. Her nose retreated, and her ears tucked in to make her more streamlined. Her skin thickened and changed texture, the fat changing to blubber, the water no longer freezing cold but more like the air up above.

Jet laughed, twisted, spun through the water, and then burst into tears.

Amber caught up with her and threw her arms around her, hushing her and petting her with her hands and her hair. "There we go, you're all right. You're back, see? All safe." She leaned away, holding Jet's shoulders. "Ready to go home?"

CHAPTER SEVENTEEN

Tessa couldn't stand it. She couldn't be in that house anymore and watch Jet leave her life as abruptly as she'd come into it. She wasn't strong enough at that moment. Hannah would be so fucking vindicated. Tessa did what she always did. She ran away.

She drove as far into the moors as she could, trying to keep the tide back, wiping tears away angrily. When they started flowing too fast, she pulled over onto the yellowing grass by the side of the road and gave up.

She'd always felt her emotions were too much, too big, too inconvenient: the anger that had nearly overwhelmed her as a teenager, the grief that had her hyperventilating in class while the rest of the family seemed to be able to show theirs in a more appropriate way. Hannah had told everyone at school that it was because she was a twin; she had that pseudo-psychic connection with Gabe. She'd sounded sympathetic, but when they were alone, she'd said, "You're not the only one who misses them, stop being attention-seeking. Do you know how embarrassing it is to get called out of your A-level classes to sort out your little sister because she can't control herself?"

And here she was doing it again. She'd known Jet for less than three weeks, and here she was, sobbing in the middle of the bloody moors over her.

At last, she managed to get herself under control and stepped out of the car for some fresh air. The wind had picked up now evening was starting to fall, and it whipped patterns over the pale green grass. The heather had turned from its summer purples to a rust brown, mottling the hills. Tessa leaned back against her car bonnet and sniffed, wiping the last of her shameful tears away.

By the time she got back to Whitby, Jet would be gone. Tessa would be alone again. She knew she was being overdramatic. Her sisters would both agree on that. Tessa had always taken things to heart. But right now, her sisters weren't there, and Tessa was sick of it all. Sick of being poised, of controlling her overwhelming emotions, of having her heart broken every time she stopped trying to hold people at arm's length. She was damn-well going to stand in the wind on the moors and be a bloody Brontë character for a bit.

The house was dark and quiet by the time she got home, the spare key she'd shoved in Amber's hand sitting on the doormat. Tessa looked at it for a long time, then turned and walked down to the seafront.

She managed to hold her emotions at bay while she went to the off-license and bought a bottle of red, and by the time she'd got to Jet's beach hut, they were almost muted, sunk deep into the mental haze Tessa had perfected over the years. She ran her fingers along the inside of the eaves out front, found the key, and unlocked the hut.

She didn't know what she'd expected. The last time she'd been here, she'd been shivering with cold and listening to Amber and Jet bicker. Amber had insisted on making the stop at the beach hut to get some towels, which mermaids apparently kept stashed for when they had land business, along with a change of clothes in case they didn't like the ones the fucking *magic* made for them.

Jet, of course, hadn't known about mildew, and Amber had had a go at her there and then before doing some magic—again, fucking *magic*—had cleaned them all up.

Handy.

Tessa was still standing in the doorway. All of Jet's stuff was here, or at least, most of the physical objects Tessa associated with her. She supposed that her real stuff was under the sea somewhere, back in Atlantis or Fairyland or whatever it was because none of this evoked Jet at all. She twisted the cap off the cheap bottle of wine and started drinking.

She ended up sitting with her legs dangling off the edge of the concrete walkway in front of the row of beach huts, staring out to sea as she drank. She could hear voices drifting down the beach, the sounds of a town getting on with life while she drank and mourned.

Not just for the loss of a woman, a possible girlfriend, but for someone who'd listened when she'd talked about boring stuff like work and surfing. For someone who'd trusted her enough to talk about her past and her vulnerabilities and encouraged her to tell her own.

And, about halfway down the bottle, for everything else she'd lost and couldn't seem to stop needing. For her mum and her twin and even her dad. He might still be there, but he was being taken away from her piece by piece in front of her eyes.

Fuck, she was a mess. She reached for the bottle and peeled off the label, staring at the last dregs through blurry vision. Maybe it was for the best that Jet was gone. At least Tessa hadn't had time to fall in love with her and watch her get fed up with all of Tessa's too-big issues and overwhelming emotions and finally leave when it could have broken her even more.

Tessa leaned her head against the railing and cried a little more.

CHAPTER EIGHTEEN

Jet didn't know what she'd been expecting on her return to Farn Deeps, but it wasn't for her father to meet her right at the edge of the caverns. He threw himself at her and wrapped her up so tight, she could barely breathe. "Dad…Dad, I'm here, I'm okay."

He moved back, freeing his hands. "What were you thinking?" he demanded in sign language. "How many times have we told you to wait for backup?"

"I'm gonna go get Auntie," Amber murmured, cocking her thumb over her shoulder.

Jet didn't stop her. She deserved this. "I'm sorry, Dad," she said. "I was…I was angry, and worked up, and—"

"I thought my last conversation with my daughter was going to be nothing but hard words and a resentment that she won't admit to." He turned away and to her horror, swiped at his eyes.

"Dad, no, please," she begged, and grabbed him in a tight hug. He clung to her for a long time, then tapped her shoulder so she'd lean back to read his signs.

"I know it's been hard for you."

She shook her head. "It's been much harder for you and Mam. I'm not blind—"

"Let me finish. All of us have to deal with memories of the war hanging over us, but you've got it in front of you every day."

He gestured at his face, the mask that protected his damaged mouth. "But I need you to get it into your head. I have never wanted revenge."

She turned her face, guilt and grief and an old, sullen anger poisoning her. Dad gently tugged her chin back so she'd look at him again. "Please, Jet. I want peace. For all of us, Knarr as well. It's not their fault."

"It's *literally* their fault. Who else could it be? Nobody else broke your fucking jaw off."

"Because it was *war.* You think I didn't cause pain? You think I didn't kill?"

Jet opened her mouth, but the words wouldn't come. He'd never talked about this before. It should've been obvious; it was war, as he'd said. But it hadn't been. It had been her sweet, funny dad whose voice she'd never heard because someone had taken it away from him. In her mind, he'd never been at fault.

"Give me some credit, Jet. I wasn't a child. I was a soldier. I should have talked about it before, and for that, I'm sorry. I should have been braver."

"You're the bravest person I've ever known."

He grimaced. "Then I definitely should have done better. Maybe if I'd spoken about the war a bit more, you'd have been slower to seek it out."

Jet's heart clenched, and she looked down. "I'm sorry, Dad. I was trying to keep us safe. I thought they were preparing to attack."

He sighed. "I know," he signed when she looked up. "You were doing what you thought best." He squeezed her arm. "Come on, let's go find your mother."

She was dreading seeing Mam most of all, but when they arrived back at Farn Deeps, Mam grabbed her wordlessly and held on tight. Amber hovered beside her, and the rest of their people were waiting, giving them space but ominously quiet. "Chief Vander is arriving tomorrow," Mam said. Jet glanced over at Amber, who was looking more anxious than she'd seen before. "He'll be early, but it'd show good faith to meet on his terms, all things considered."

"All things..."

"One of the Knarr you fought has died," Amber said. "Gul... he was fine when I left, I swear. I thought he was going to make a full recovery but...it must have been an infection."

Jet felt her heart sink, stone-like, and bile rose in her throat. She swallowed it hard. She'd killed someone.

When she was a youngster, she'd imagined fighting great battles, winning glorious victories, ensuring the enemy, the Knarr, never got to hurt her people again. But the reality of what that would mean had never really occurred to her. She remembered the taste of blood in her gills, the feel of her spear driving deep into the tail of one of the Knarr, the shouts and screams, the terror, the cuts that still pulled at her skin.

They wouldn't pull on his skin anymore. The faceless enemy of her childhood games had a name now. He'd probably had a family.

Mam squeezed her wrist, and when Jet met her gaze, she saw understanding there. A knowledge her parents had wanted to keep from her, and now she saw why. *Nobody should ever know this.*

❖

Swimming around Farn Deeps felt like a dream, like a distant memory. Something nostalgic and pure, and she'd tainted it with the blood on her hands.

She found herself slinking deep into the labyrinth of caves by the healing rooms. She hadn't realised she'd been going that way, but it made a twisted sort of sense.

"I know you're out there, Jet," called Marra.

Jet sighed and swam forward with a kick of her tail. The old mermaid was at her workstation, grinding a pot of some medicine or other. Jet had never been interested in how she made her remedies. That probably said everything anyone needed to know about her, she thought guiltily.

Marra looked up at her and pointed at a space laid out on the floor. "I should be transcribing those notes into the database," she said. "Give an old lady a hand?"

Jet gave her a tired half-smile and sank to the floor to type the information into the system, her tail flicking constantly to hold her in place against the sand. Tessa would have found the database fascinating, she realised with a painful jab of memory. She would have wanted someone to explain exactly how the energy was transported to their system, whether they used wires or pipes or batteries. But Tessa was on land, safe away from Jet, and Jet was a murderer.

There was movement in the hallway, and Jet flicked her tail and shoved herself up with her arms as someone came in. "Miss Marra, excuse me, I came to ask for—"

The merman caught sight of Jet and trailed off, his body tensing. She recognised him at the same time; he'd been the leader in their fight back in the buffer zone. Brede, she remembered.

"I'll come back later," he said and turned.

"Wait, no, please."

He paused in the entranceway and side-eyed her. "I can go," she said, gesturing at Marra. "I was just hiding out, I guess. You stay."

He turned completely and regarded her, his expression guarded, his tail twitching and betraying his agitation. It made her want to fidget, which in turn made her angry at herself, which made her feel guilty.

"You're Jet," he said at last.

She nodded. "I, uh…I heard about your friend."

"Gul."

She ducked her head. “I’m sorry. I—” She bit back the rest of the words. They all sounded like excuses, and none of them sounded like enough. He probably didn’t want to hear them anyway. “I’m sorry.”

The water shifted around her, and when she looked up, he was gone. She slumped. She didn’t know what she’d expected or hoped to achieve.

“Come on, lass,” said Marra, her voice soft. “Them notes won’t write themselves.”

She drifted back down through the still water, stretching out onto the triangular cushion they used to prop themselves up for things like writing. She wondered idly what Tessa would think about this, now, about the lack of chairs. It made her sad.

“How do you fix a thing like this?” she asked Marra.

“You don’t,” she said, pressing a button on the machine and lifting the round pot of medicine out. “Things like this, it’s like growing a plant. You’ve given your apology, planted your seed, and now you got to leave it to grow. Sometimes it can, sometimes it can’t, but if you keep digging it up to see if it’s worked, you’re going to kill it.”

She sighed, pushing a tiny stream of bubbles out of the corner of her lips. “I don’t like not being able to fix things.”

“Nobody does.” Marra sank to the ground across from Jet with a grunt. “It’s one of the reasons a thing like this is so big, so terrible. There’s no fixing it. Only healing, if you can.”

She nodded, a lump growing in her throat and nearly choking her. “I wish there was something I could do. I wish…I wish I’d never hurt anyone.” She remembered the taste of blood again, the way it had clogged her gills. She pressed her hand to her mouth, tears rising in her eyes and floating into the sea.

“I know,” said Marra, and rubbed the back of her hand. “I know.”

❖

She lay curled between her parents that night like a little child, trying to pretend she wasn't crying.

Mam stroked her shoulder. "It's all right, love," she said, and from the thickness of her voice, Jet knew she was crying too. "We won't let them take you."

"Maybe I deserve it," Jet whispered. "I deserve whatever they want to do to me."

"No," said Dad, shifting so both his hands were free to sign. "I'm not saying you don't need to atone for what you did, but Vander is…he won't be fair."

"Halligen," said Mam, a warning.

Dad rose to sign clearly to both of them. "It's time she knew, Cordelia. If we'd told her before, maybe this wouldn't have happened."

"Knew what?" said Jet, twitching her tail to push her up into a sitting position against the headboard. Her heart was beating hard, afraid of more upheaval.

"I am Knarr," Dad signed, and Jet's jaw dropped.

"You are *not* Knarr," said Mam, her voice thick with distress. "They turned their back on you."

"You could say that I turned my back on them just as much," he said, his signs sharp and sweeping.

Mam pushed herself up and swam away. Dad watched, his eyes sad. Jet barely noticed. Her father was Knarr. Her own dad. "I've…I've hated them my whole life, and you…"

Dad sighed. "I didn't want to talk about it."

"I hated them for what they did to you, and the whole time, it was for nothing?"

Silence fell between them. Jet's words seemed to echo with her grief and shame. She swallowed hard. "Tell me."

"I was the chief's advisor. Havso, that was his name. We'd been fighting so long, not just the Knarr and Farn Deeps, but all the mer clans. The Hatton were at war with the Rockall for decades. Humber were fighting both us *and* the Knarr at one point about a hundred years ago. We're more like humans than you think, always fighting each other."

"How did you change sides?" she asked, though her throat felt like she'd been screaming for hours.

"I met your mam," he said. He wasn't looking at her, concentrating on his hands, as if that would protect him from her reactions. "I was netting mackerel and got netted myself." He huffed a little laugh. "The humans' nets are a lot more effective. I was so focused on what I was doing that I didn't realise how close their trawlers were getting. Stupid. But your mother, she saved me. Cut that net right open to drag me out, then called me an idiot in so many ways, you'd have thought she'd run out of insults."

"Did you know, then? That she was your enemy?"

"Of course," he said. "She knew, too. She'd known when she saw me scooped up by that trawler." He rubbed his forehead. "Jet, I did a lot of things I'm not proud of. Before that and after. Your mother doesn't see it this way, but I betrayed my people."

"You spied on them?"

"No, not really. I took a while to make my decision. It was a big choice. Her or everyone else, you know? But when I did leave to be with her, I took everything I knew about the Knarr with me. And Havso believed to the end that I'd been a spy, actively working to bring them down."

Jet wiped her eyes. "Why are you telling me this now? How does it help?"

Dad closed his eyes as if steeling himself. "Because Havso was Vander's big brother, and I killed him." He gestured to his jaw. "We fought for the end of the war, the two of us, and though Vander was bound to accept the outcome, though Havso nearly killed me too, he will never forgive. He will always be looking for his chance for revenge. I should have told you before."

"Why didn't you?"

"Your mam and I thought we could keep you away from all of it. We thought we could put it behind us and move on."

Jet fought and lost against her grief. "How can we move on, Dad? Until we have all the information, how can we know how to?"

She pressed her hands to her eyes and sobbed. Dad put his hand on her shoulder tentatively, then around her back, and she leaned into him for a moment. But every touch felt like shark skin, tiny teeth biting into her and tearing her apart, until she had to push away and swim into the dark.

CHAPTER NINETEEN

Tucked into one of the high nooks on a nearby ridge, Jet slept fitfully. She woke before sunrise and lay on her stomach, watching the sunbeams through the water with aching eyes. She tugged the sleeves of Tessa's hoodie down over her hands and pressed her face against the soft, too-thick material, trying to seek out what little comfort remained after the magic and ocean water had washed through it.

What could she do? Marra was right; there was no fixing something like this. She'd seen so many mer her parents' age and older still haunted by the blood they'd spilled, and she'd thought, somehow, that it was all someone else's fault. How could it be her own people? Her own people were all kind, irritating, silly, smart, and loving. She knew each one, and none of them was evil.

And her dad. Her sweet, funny dad, who'd spent her whole childhood in pain, recovering from infection after infection, sedated for surgeries and grafts and whatever else Marra could devise to keep him around and improve his quality of life little by little. He'd killed people. He'd turned on people. He'd been born a Knarr, one of the clan she hated, even when her parents had told her not to. In hindsight, it was so obvious. Even his black and grey tail was clearly Knarr. She would laugh at herself if the lump in her throat could ever allow it.

There was no going back from this, but Jet couldn't stagnate either. That wouldn't bring Gul back or Vander's brother or her dad's health. Or any of the other lives that had been lost in the war.

Slowly, she wriggled out of the nook and dropped through the cold morning water, swimming low to the seafloor on her way back to Farn Deeps. The sand beneath her tail puffed up in clouds like it always had. Flatfish and prawns skittered out of her way like they always had. Life went on. She had to as well.

The only other choice was to sink. Jet thought wryly of Tessa and the number she'd left in the hut for the Samaritans. She thought maybe now she understood what Tessa had been trying to say, but Jet was selfish and a survivor. She'd rather swim on with the weight of Gul's soul alongside her than sink and join him. She wondered what that said about her.

Dad and Mam were bent together, both signing sharply, hiding their conversation from the rest of the community. Jet swam up and hugged them both tightly, feeling the moment of uncertainty before they hugged her back just as tightly, as if they could hold themselves together with force of will.

"It's time," Mam said, leaning back and cupping Jet's cheek. She let Jet and Dad go and turned to one of the men nearby. "Loph, will you tell Vander we'll meet with him at the Ring in one hour?"

Loph nodded, his usual teasing smile nowhere to be seen. He and another young lad swam off into the haze, while Mam, Amber, and Jet made their way to the Ring.

The natural amphitheater of the Ring had always been a meeting place for the clans from this part of the North Sea, and Amber in particular had a hand in keeping it maintained. The circle of rock had long been covered with a carefully curated kelp forest, leaving a clearing in the middle into which the sunlight filtered down like a benediction. Even as a child, Jet had felt the majesty of this place, and she'd only sneaked into the clearing once, on a dare. She'd swum through the great plants, the awe building in her, and when she'd burst into the open space bathed in shafts of light, she'd been unable to move for a moment, overwhelmed by the sanctity of it. Where they lived, there were so few enclosed spaces that this felt holy somehow. It was no wonder their people held peace talks here. Even a child could feel the hope, the expectation of making a better world.

She told the boys who'd dared her to go in that she hadn't gotten there. She'd taken the forfeit rather than admit she'd broken the sanctity of the Ring.

Mam turned to her, and Jet was sure she was going to say something, but the Knarr arrived.

Chief Vander was a little younger than Mam and Dad, and he radiated fury. He swam straight to the smaller ring of sugar kelp growing right in the centre of the Ring. Mam and Jet approached too, as did two of the other Knarr. They always seemed to do things in threes. It was a tradition of theirs which Jet had never cared to understand. Brede was one of the three. Jet looked away and resisted the urge to beg his forgiveness. It wasn't hers to take.

As Amber, Loph, and the rest of the Knarr delegation retreated back through the dense kelp forest, those who remained reached out and grasped a clump of sugar kelp with their weapon hand. Only then did the talks begin.

"Is this her?" Vander asked, tilting his head toward Brede while jerking his chin at Jet.

Brede looked at her, his expression guarded but not only from her. "Yes, sir."

"Like mother, like daughter," Vander said to Mam, and though she'd heard it before, it wasn't usually sneered quite this much.

"And here I thought *ad hominem* attacks were beneath a meeting in the Ring. Yes, Vander, this is my daughter, returned from land as Amber promised."

"She is a murderer, and yet, I don't see her in chains."

"It was not murder. If anything, it was self-defense. Your men attacked first."

"So claims another Farn, her cousin, no less. How can we trust that?"

"It is true," Brede said, putting his left hand up, then dropping it and looking away when Vander turned to glare at him. "I only…it was more complicated than that."

"Please, explain?" Mam said, her voice gentler than it had been with Vander.

Brede glanced at Jet, then Vander. Jet noticed he had chosen a handful of sugar kelp a step away from Vander, not directly beside him as the other Knarr had done on the other side of their leader. "It was an accident," Brede said, now speaking to Jet. "Haj is only young, and he's traumatised. He thought your cousin, the wi…the mage, excuse me, was attacking. I tried to stop him, but…"

"But I went off on a hair trigger," Jet said quietly.

Brede hesitated, then nodded.

"I am sorry for your friend. For Gul." She swallowed, but the words would barely come out above a whisper. "I'm sorry."

"Sorry is not enough," Vander said, his hand gripping the sugar kelp so tightly, it was a wonder it didn't tear right through. "Did we not have a treaty? Did you Farn not decimate our people enough in the war, you have to train your young to kill ours?"

"That's enough," Mam snapped.

"It was enough when the war ended," Vander all but roared. "It would be enough to use diplomacy instead of throwing us back into battle. This…this forced apology is nothing."

"It's not forced," Jet said, her temper rising. She swallowed it back and calmed herself. "I'm not faking it. I am genuinely sorry, and I'll do what I can to make it right."

"How can you make it right?" Vander slapped the palm of his hand on his armoured chest plate in emphasis. "One of our own is dead by your hand. Do you purpose to bring him back? Or give your own life in recompense?"

Mam leaped forward at that, and almost at the same time, Vander's hand left his sugar kelp. The two of them, a hair's breadth from snatching at each other's throats, were blasted out of the Ring by the magic. Jet had just enough of her senses about her to cling on tighter, her arm over her face as the ancient magic howled around her, kicking up sand from the seafloor to scour her skin.

When it passed, she looked up, meeting the wide eyes of the two remaining Knarr. The one who'd been on Vander's right released his own sugar kelp, backing away slowly as if expecting the Ring to attack him for it. As soon as he was a few tail kicks away, he turned and swam, probably to find Vander.

"Did you know it would do that?" asked Brede.

Jet shook her head. "No, I swear. We all know the Ring has its own magic to keep the peace, but I always thought it was more…metaphorical." She glanced up at the clearing fog of kicked-up sand. "Should've guessed, though, really."

Brede followed her gaze up. "Where are they, do you think? Are they okay?"

"Probably just outside the kelp forest?" She looked back at him. "Look, Brede, honestly. I am so sorry. I know that doesn't help, but…"

"No," he said. "It doesn't, not really." It wasn't cruel, just sad, matter-of-fact. He sighed as if in defeat. "We shouldn't have been that close."

"Why were you there?" It came out pleading, like knowing would somehow make things different, bring Gul back. "Amber said you had to get away from the noises, but why there? It's not like your chief wasn't involved in setting up the borderlines."

"He's not my chief." Brede's voice was suddenly hard, not angry, but firm. The unyielding tone took Jet by surprise, and she tilted her head, curious despite herself. Brede glanced behind him. "He won't change," he said, dropping his voice. "He insists on staying in Fiskebank, and for what? Some sort of loyalty to the seafloor there?"

"And you want to..."

"We want to leave, find somewhere we can hunt again, somewhere we won't get those *sounds*. We can't keep doing it."

"What do they sound like?" she asked.

"You don't hear them? I can still hear them sometimes, but at least here, it's distant, you know? In Fiskebank, it was like a blow to the head. So loud some of us got sick. Not many of us." He shrugged. "Vander was one of those who could stand it. He said it was nothing more than an inconvenience. But all of us, all those you saw in the settlement...we're not malingering. We cannot live there."

"You can hear them even here? I don't hear anything."

Brede's shoulders slumped slightly. "You don't believe me, either."

"That's not it," she said quickly. "I'm thinking of solutions. You know what causes it, right? The sonar?"

"It's the humans. Certain ships of theirs, not all of them. We don't know what they're doing. Not that it matters. We have little to do with them, unlike you Farn."

Jet looked away, her thoughts going straight to Tessa against her will. Then, her eyes snapped wide. "We can ask."

Brede snorted. "Sure, we'll go up to the nearest human and ask them to stop because their actions are harming us. Haven't you heard the stories? Don't the old ones teach the little Farn why we keep ourselves a secret? Humans don't care about their own. Why would they care for us when they think we're a myth?"

"No, I know that won't work. We've all seen the wrecks of their warships. But I know someone who does this. She understands how it works, how *people* work. She was talking to me about some sonar technology the humans have to search for oil under the seafloor, how it's affecting whales who hunt with sonar. It might be the same thing that's hurting your people."

"You *know* a human?" He frowned at her, almost literally looking down his nose.

"It's a long story. Yes. I…I know her well."

"And she knows…"

"Yeah." Jet nodded. "She knows about merfolk."

He considered for a moment, then shook his head. "Even if she knows about the sounds and wants to help, what can she do?"

"I don't know, but she might know a way to make them stop. And if she doesn't…well, maybe she'll know a way to break the machinery."

He tilted his head. "Sabotage? I thought you liked humans."

"I like one human," she said. "They're not all the same, you know. They're individuals, not a hive mind."

"Ah," he said, nodding. "A little how not all Knarr are warmongering invaders who think of nothing but how to kill all the Farn Deepers?"

Jet's cheeks flushed hot, and she glared. "Oh, you mean some are?"

He shrugged. "I don't pretend to know what all my people are thinking."

"Touché. Okay then, what do you think? Are you willing to give it a try?"

"Talking to your friendly human? I don't know how I'd go about it."

She bit her lip, now in her element when developing a plan of attack. "We'll need Amber and another of these amulets," she said, touching the stone that still hung around her neck. "The three of us can shift into human form and find Tessa, tell her the problem, and go from there."

"Human form? All of us?"

"I mean, unless you want her to come have a chat with you waist-deep in water where any passing surfer can see your tail?"

"No, thank you," he said, shuddering. "You're ready to escape, then?"

"What?" She frowned, cocking her head on one side. "What are you talking about?"

He raised an eyebrow. "Do you think you'll be allowed to go on this field trip freely? Vander wants you executed, preferably in Fiskebank."

"He what?" She gaped at him.

"Are you surprised? He was second-in-command in the last war against your mother. His brother died because of your family."

"Right," she said. "Well, shit." For a moment, she thought about it. Would this be her punishment? Should she let justice take its course? "Do you even want me to take you?"

He looked at her, exhaustion deep in his eyes. "What other option do we have? Keep scraping a living in the buffer zone, attacked by both sides for being freaks or enemies? Or move onto someone else's land and see how they take it?"

"I'm sorry," she said, her voice small.

"Do you really think I care about Vander's vendetta? I just want my people to be able to live and eat, and if that means making a treaty with one enemy, it's one more treaty than we had before."

"Even though I killed one of you?"

His eyes hardened. "Vander has allowed tens of us to die, pushing us to go out and hunt while the sounds nearly broke our skulls, then calling us cowards when we were vomiting blood. I wouldn't stand by him by choice, even against you. The only reason I'm here is to give my people time to pack up and leave."

Jet let that sink in, then set her jaw. "Right, well, I think we can do better than that. My debt is to you, not that arsehole. Escape it is."

He looked down at the kelp. "If we release this, will we be thrown out?"

"The other Knarr was fine when he let go," she said. Even so, she couldn't help but brace herself as she let go, trying to look confident. "There. See?" She grinned at Brede, who raised an eyebrow, unimpressed, and followed her out of the kelp forest, retrieving their weapons on the way.

When Amber grabbed her arm as they emerged, Jet almost stabbed her. "What were you thinking?" Jet demanded.

"Shh, shut up. We need to go." Amber glanced up at Brede and did a double-take. "What, are you two friends, now?"

"We need to go talk to Tessa. I'll explain on the way. Do you have an extra amulet?"

"I'm way ahead of you. Vander and Auntie Cordelia had a huge fight. He says if you're not punished, they're going to attack. I think his advisors are trying to find a way out of it, but he's not backing down. And honestly, Auntie's not helping with the way she keeps calling him a coward. You need to lie low. I'm thinking you get back on land, and we'll make a plan of action there."

Brede shrugged. "Well, our intentions line up."

Jet nodded. "I need to take Brede with me. We need to talk to Tessa about sonar. I can't bring Gul back, but we might be able to find a way to make things better for Brede's clan."

"*Brede's* clan? Jet, are you starting a fucking coup?"

"No, it's not like that, it's—"

Brede's gaze snapped to the side. "We have to leave, now. They're coming."

Amber frowned at him. "How can you…"

"Can you not hear?"

"Fuck, come *on*," Jet said, dragging the two of them, her tail already beating hard. She had a momentary twang of guilt for leaving again so quickly. Her parents would be terrified for her, especially with all this tension. But this was bigger than her now.

Chapter Twenty

Tessa regretted all her life choices on Monday morning. She was too old to be getting drunk on a Sunday night, especially as she was pretty sure her tolerance had taken a hit since her uni years. One bottle of wine hadn't been enough to make her feel this bad ten years ago.

Not that things had usually stopped with one bottle back then, so maybe it was an unfair comparison.

She dragged herself to work, almost grateful for the bracing wind startling her awake. She deliberately didn't look at the sea. It was time to turn her back on mermaids and other sorts of wishful thinking. She had her job; that was enough. It would have to be. There was even a bitter part of her that pointed out that at least *these* were *her* people.

She was the first to arrive, unlocking the door and flicking on the lights, starting up the coffee machine. She hadn't been the first one at work for a few weeks. Since Jet had turned up and distracted her.

She shook the thought off and started up her computer, opening up the presentation for the meeting with the fisheries commission and letting herself get lost in ideas and strategies. She'd spent years trying *not* to get this lost, and for what? Because Hannah thought she should spend more time with family? Because Joanie said it made her boring? Right now, it was the only thing reminding her that she actually had a purpose in life.

The fisheries project was important. It was common knowledge that fish stocks were decreasing all the time and that the quotas were an essential part of preventing overfishing. In theory. In practice, it was next to impossible to target one particular species with something like a net, and any fish like cod caught over the quota were thrown back into the sea, often already dead.

Tessa didn't want to be part of the problem, preaching to people who worked in dangerous conditions and who already felt disenfranchised. She wanted to find some way of getting suggestions from the trawlermen themselves rather than telling them what to do, and that was going to be a challenge. Guys like that were understandably suspicious of outsiders, and she didn't have an in with them. This was what she needed to focus on, the perfect thing to get her mind off Jet.

A sharp click to her left made her startle violently. "Sorry," said Sophie, hand still on the coffee mug she'd put on Tessa's desk. "You were really in the zone there, huh?"

Tessa rubbed tension out of her forehead. "Yeah, trying to work out the best way to deal with the fisheries job. Good weekend?"

Sophie dived into an anecdote about David meeting her new puppy, complete with video footage on her phone. Tessa told herself she was happy for her and not at all jealous that her coworkers were all loved up, and she had just lost the woman of her dreams because she wasn't *her people*. She sat back and sipped her coffee and smiled in all the right places and cooed over the sweet selfie of Sophie and the new puppy sitting on David's lap.

The landline on Tessa's desk started to ring, and both she and Sophie startled and stared at it, then at each other. "I didn't think that was even connected anymore," Tessa murmured.

"Maybe it's a cold caller."

Tessa shrugged and picked up. "GreenSTAR, Tessa Bordeaux speaking."

"Tessa, love? It's Dad."

Tessa's heart thumped around her chest like it couldn't decide what to do. Dad was calling. He'd remembered her name and number. An obscure one but still. But Dad was calling… "Is everything okay? Where are you?"

"Everything's fine, duck. But there's a little lad here who says you're his auntie?"

Tessa frowned. "What?"

The phone crackled, and voices murmured in the background. "Aunt Tessa?" Ben said, sniffing.

"Ben? What are you doing at Granddad's place? Where's your mum?"

"I don't want to see her. I hate her."

"What? But—no, hold on. I'll be right there, you hear? Don't move, either of you. Are you in Granddad's room?"

"No, we're in the reception. They wouldn't let me go see Granddad without Mum or Dad here, so he had to come up. I'm not sorry."

"That's fine. Just stay there, okay?"

Tessa hung up and stood, bashing her hip on the table. "Shit. Soph, I've got to go, family emergency, I'm sorry."

"Of course," she said, her eyes wide and worried. "Don't worry about a thing. I'll tell Andy."

She picked up her bag and started to log off her computer at the same time. "Shit. The fisheries document, I should put that on the shared drive. And there's the rundown from Pontegrass—"

"Tessa, we love you, but I'm sure we'll cope." Sophie raised her eyebrows and gave her a fond little smile. "You've trained us well, now go."

Tessa let out a long breath. "Okay. Yeah. Okay, but call me if you need anything."

"We won't need anything we can't fix ourselves, now, go sort your family out."

Tessa shook her head and huffed, but Sophie was right. They were all good at their roles. She snatched her coat off the hook by the door, mumbled an apology to Elias and Andy at the door when she nearly bowled them over, and ran.

By the time she'd run home to get her car, then driven to Dad's home, she had worked the drama up in her mind into something terrible, a domino effect of tragedy that Hannah would blame her for and from which she'd never recover. When she burst into the reception and saw a couple of the nurses having tea and biscuits with her dad and nephew, she burst into tears.

"Oh, Tessa, love, come here," Dad said, standing and struggling with his crutch to get to her.

"How about we get you three a bit of privacy?" one of the nurses said at the edge of Tessa's awareness. They were bustled into a room with lumpy sofas, and somehow, Tessa ended up in the middle. Dad sat on one side with his leg propped out in front of him in its supportive boot, and Ben sat on her other side, his arms wrapped tightly around her.

"I'm just glad you're okay," she said at last.

"Of course we are, why wouldn't we be?" Dad said, rubbing her shoulder with a fond chuckle. "Always so serious, our Tess."

She wanted to scream in frustration because this could all have been serious. It was no laughing matter. But she also wanted to curl up against Dad and soak up his lucidity. He hadn't stayed present for this long in years.

She wiped her eyes and pulled herself together. First, she had to find out what was going on. "Ben, what happened?"

"I don't want to see Mum," he said, his face pressed into her side.

"Why?" she asked. He grumbled unintelligibly. "C'mon, I need to know. Can you tell me what happened this morning?"

He sighed and sat back a bit. "She told me I can't go see you anymore because you're a bad influence."

Tessa's laugh burst from her in surprise. "I am? Why, what did I do this time?"

Ben sat up properly and crossed his arms, glowering at nothing, and mumbled.

"I can't hear, Ben."

"I said she's being racist, okay?"

Tessa's mouth dropped open. "Huh?"

"She said you hanging around with *mermaids* is bad, and she said it like that, you know? What's wrong with other types of people? She's like those people Dad warned me about. No wonder she never wanted him to talk about it with me, but Dad says it's important for people of colour and biracial people like me to know about racists young, to know what to stay away from."

"Ben, I don't think—"

"And I know it's not real. I'm not dumb. I know Jet's just playing at being a mermaid because she doesn't want to say where she's really from, but it's the way she said it. Like, 'I don't want you hanging out with *that mermaid* girl, I want you to stay away from Auntie Tessa because she's exposing you to bad influences.' I was so mad with her. I didn't say anything, but when she dropped me at school, I turned around and left. I didn't even go in. I was gonna come to yours, but Granddad's was closer, so…what are you laughing about? It's not funny!"

Tessa covered her face, her shoulders shaking. "I'm sorry. I'm not laughing at you. She's not being racist, I promise."

"Well, what the hell—"

"She's being homophobic." Tessa giggled into her hands. "God, what a defence that is."

"What do you mean?"

Tessa wiped her eyes, the hysteria subsiding slightly. "She thinks *mermaid* is some sort of code for lesbian. She thinks I'm going to make you gay or something." She snorted and dropped her face back into her hands.

Ben was quiet for a moment. "I don't think that's how being gay works, Tessa," he said gently.

Tessa burst into more giggles. "You're right," she said when she could get control over herself again. "It's not, but sometimes, people think it is." She shrugged sadly and looked over at her dad. "Sorry. You were never supposed to find out."

"Find out what, love?"

"That I'm gay."

Dad shrugged and patted her on the shoulder. "Oh, don't worry about that. One of my daughters is gay, my wife says."

Tessa froze. "What?"

He nodded and smiled. "I've got twins," he said. "My middle children, they just started secondary school, and the little lass, Tessa, she's practically in love with one of her classmates."

"Granddad, that is—"

Tessa hushed Ben. "You…you knew?"

"Well, no, my wife was the one who noticed and told me." He put his hand on her shoulder and squeezed gently, reassuringly. "Now look, it took a bit of getting used to, but that's just because I want her to be happy, like all my children. Your parents will want the same, I'm sure. And if they don't, well, you come tell me, won't you? What's your name again, love?"

Tessa didn't reply, just threw herself at her dad and wrapped her arms tight around him, the tears she'd thought she'd pressed down safe flooding out again. Dad patted her on the back. "There, there, love, it's all right. Gabe, why don't you go get this lady some tea, and we'll set the world to rights."

She heard Ben stand, his small hand briefly stroking her hair before the door clicked shut. Tessa cried for relief and sorrow, knowing that Dad would probably forget all this in minutes. She cried for years of shame and hiding and of the bittersweetness of knowing that her mum had figured it out just before she'd died and what could have been if she'd been around. She cried for her mum and her brother and the shattered remains of her family left behind.

Eventually, she asked the reception to call Hannah. Maybe she should have done that before. Maybe the fact that she wasn't a mum and didn't want to be made her selfish, but she was glad she hadn't gotten hold of her until Ben had had a chance to explain. Not that Hannah would see it that way, she thought bitterly.

"I don't want to see her," Ben said, but it was a resigned petulance. He knew none of them had much of a choice in the matter.

"I know," said Tessa. "I'll speak to her on your behalf, but I doubt it'll make her happy. She thinks I'm a bad influence anyway."

Ben slumped. "I've made it worse."

Tessa hugged him. "Not for me," she said. "I'm proud of you, you know. You saw injustice, and you made a stand against it. But remember, you're still young, okay? Your first priority is your own safety."

"I was safe, though. It's not like I ran here or anything. I caught a bus."

"Yeah, by yourself," she said.

He sighed. "Being a kid sucks."

"You don't have a lot of power over your life, I know. But you will soon enough, okay? Don't rush the process."

He rolled his eyes and almost certainly didn't listen, as was the way of children. She watched him slouch over and sit next to his Granddad, listening to a story he'd told him several times before. Ben was kind and patient in a way Hannah probably had been once, before things all went to shit and made her the designated mother of the family.

Her phone pinged with a message from Elias. *Hope your dad's okay.*

Thanks, she sent back, her chest warming with affection for her team. *Everyone's fine, I should be back in later.*

Andy says, don't you dare!

Tessa laughed and sent a string of amused emoji back before tucking her phone away. Dad was on the second retelling of the same story, and Ben was looking a little glassy-eyed when the front door of the facility slammed open.

"Ah, shit," Tessa muttered. Hannah's high heels were stomping loud enough for them to hear down the corridor, tucked in their little meeting room, and though she wasn't in full indignation mode yet, Tessa could hear the tone of her voice as she spoke to the receptionist.

Ben slumped in his seat. "She's gonna be so mad."

"Yup."

She was. But Tessa saw the flicker of a deeper truth the moment Hannah walked into the room. She recognised that same terror in her sister's eyes, the worst that could possibly happen, that had already happened once. No matter what people said, you had to see the evidence of safety with your own eyes.

"What on earth were you thinking?" Hannah demanded of Ben. "Do you have any idea how dangerous that was, how much trouble you've caused for everyone? Well?"

Ben shrank and shrugged, his lower lip starting to protrude.

"Answer me, Benjamin."

"Hannah, he was—"

Hannah put her hand up at Tessa, fast as a whip, and only then did she turn her banked fury on her. "Can I have a word with you? Outside?"

Tessa resisted the urge to groan and followed her out. Hannah turned the moment the door slipped shut behind them, standing almost nose to nose with Tessa. "What are you doing here? Did they call you first? And why the hell didn't you call me as soon as you knew?"

"I'm here because—"

"And why Dad's? Honestly, I can't believe the reception didn't call me right away, I'll be lodging a complaint about this.

What is going on? And what has it got to do with you, of all people?"

Tessa raised her eyebrows.

"Well?" Hannah snapped.

"Oh, you want an answer now, do you?"

"Don't get cute with me, Tessa, I've just found out my son has run away from school for some unknown reason—"

"Maybe if you shut the fuck up once in a while, you'd find out why."

They stared at each other in shock. Tessa could hardly believe the words had left her mouth, but now they had, the anger she'd worked to hold back was bubbling under the surface, demanding to be heard. "You think you know what's best for everyone, but you don't. You're just a scared, bigoted little girl, trying to run our lives your way."

"How dare you—"

"Oh, will you shut up?" she said, her heart beating harder, all the resentment and misery that she'd denied she'd ever felt toward her big sister burning hot in her veins. "I'm done being ashamed because of you, so save your pearl clutching for someone else. I only hope you don't pass that self-loathing on to your son the way you did to me. Lucky for him, he's already wise to you. He thinks you're racist, by the way. Because of the whole 'don't hang out with mermaids' comment this morning. Great job."

"Racist? Why…what are you talking about?"

"Because he didn't think 'mermaid' was a slang word for lesbian like you seem to, you utter idiot."

Hannah almost hissed and looked around. "Keep your voice down."

Tessa laughed. It felt more like a scream, the way it hurt to come out. "Why? Do you think we're Voldemort? Are dykes going to appear like magic because I said the L-word? I fucking wish."

“Stop being stupid and selfish and think about Dad for once. What if he hears you?”

Tessa was crying now, angry tears hot on her cheeks. “You bitch. You absolute bitch. He knows.”

“He—”

“He’s known since I was a kid. Mum told him. She figured it out when I was crushing on Dani in year seven. So thanks, Hannah, because I’ve spent half my life hating myself because you were convinced it would kill Dad to know one of his girls was queer.”

“Tessa?” said Dad.

“Fuck.” Tessa turned away from the open door, away from Dad and Ben and all the nurses and everyone now gathering around staring at her sobbing in the hallway. “Fuck,” she said, shoved past Hannah, and left.

CHAPTER TWENTY-ONE

Jet led the way to land, Amber and Brede cutting through the water almost silently beside her. The three of them were tense, hands clenched in fists by their hips as they beat their tails, gill flaps beating fast, and muscles aching.

Amber was the first to tire, falling behind, then struggling to catch up and hide her exhaustion. "Fuck," Jet muttered. "Come on, not much farther."

"I'm fine," Amber said.

"We could go closer to the surface," Brede offered. "Gulp some air if necessary." Jet looked at him, her head on one side. "You know," he said, gesturing upward unnecessarily. "Air has more dissolved oxygen in it?"

"It does?"

"I…I'm pretty sure it does, yes." His voice turned up, defying his words.

"He's right," Amber said, clearly out of breath and trying to hide it. She glanced up. "I might have to…but the amulets will make your tails disappear as soon as our heads break the surface, and I don't trust human legs to keep you above the waves long enough."

Jet nodded. Inhaling water into human lungs was no fun at all. "How do you know that about the oxygen?" she asked Brede.

"Knarr have school, you know."

She rolled her eyes. "I didn't mean it like that. But *I* didn't know about the oxygen thing. I bet Amber only knows because she's a nerd."

Amber shrugged and didn't deny it.

"We often break the surface," Brede said. "When we're hunting, on long pursuits, we take turns to swim upside down and gulp air. It's not like we ever wear amulets like these, so drowning's not a problem."

"Huh," said Jet. "That's useful, I guess."

"Not something we have to do," Amber said. "We mostly gather mollusks or algae."

Brede crinkled his face up. "Boring. I don't know how you can eat such side dishes alone without meat. In our clan, we have more variety in our food."

"Don't knock it till you've tried it."

"I would rather just have the meat than just the algae." His head snapped to the side, and without warning, he stopped and made some clicking sounds in the back of his throat.

"What is it?" Amber whispered, her sensory hair spreading wide to gather vibrations.

Brede didn't reply but cupped his hands over his mouth and clicked again. Jet was sure there were other sounds he was making too, vibrations she could feel on her skin and her hair but couldn't pick up with her ears. She felt the sensation of goose bumps rising on her skin, as impossible as that was as a mermaid, and loosed her spear from her back.

Brede held his hand out to her. "It's fine. It's my clan."

"What? That's not fucking fine, Brede," said Amber, her voice high.

"I said mine. Not Vander's." His voice was almost a growl, and as he said it, a group of about ten mer materialised from the gloom like a pod of dolphin.

A smile split his face, and he rushed toward them, speaking low and quickly in Knarr. When he turned back, his face was pale. "Vander's declared me traitor."

"Not only you," said an older mermaid with a patchy grey tail. "All of us. He is no longer even pretending to avenge Gul." She met Jet's gaze steadily, and Jet couldn't help but look away.

"We all have to leave, now." Brede turned to his people, glancing from one to another. "We're lying to ourselves if we think we can stay. We have to accept that we're no longer Knarr, not to them. We are ourselves now."

"But what about—"

"I'm sorry, Jet. I have to stay with my people."

"No, but Tessa can help. I'm sure she can."

Amber nodded. "Your best chance is to escape by land." She looked around. "Where are the rest of you? There were others back in the settlement."

"They're hiding up by the ridge. We're going back for them now," Brede said, already blending into their group.

Jet had a horrifying image of Vander and his people attacking not just her own. Farn Deeps could be easily defended via catacombs of tunnels beneath the seafloor, but Brede's people were in unfamiliar waters, trying to find somewhere safe without knowing where to go. Young and old, they'd be too slow, and they would have nowhere to hide when Vander took out his rage on them too.

She looked at the pod of mer in front of her, the ferocious hunters now gaunt and hopeless but stoic for one last stand against their erstwhile leader. She'd been so afraid of them. She'd hurt them, killed one of them.

She wanted to save them too.

"I'll distract the Knarr," she said.

"You'll do what?" asked Amber, one eyebrow raised.

Jet nodded. She thought about Tessa, about how she looked at a team and let them use their strengths. "We're nearly at Whitby, and they'll figure out that's where we're going. If we can draw them off, get them to follow us to land—maybe even onto land, if necessary—then you guys will be able to get to the others, get everyone safe."

"Where will we go?" asked the woman who'd spoken before. She had a flat affect, as if she was too exhausted from failed hope to care anymore. "We should stay and fight."

Jet nodded, her mind buzzing with possibilities. "Amber, you have to take them to Farn Deeps. Get Dad on our side and Marra. The others'll follow."

"And what, hide behind the aprons of farmers?" said one of the younger Knarr.

"No." Jet pointed to him. "You won't be. Anyone who can fight, must, and that means you and us Farn Deepers."

"Surely, it's not going to come to that?" said Amber. The fact that she was asking rather than laughing off Jet's orders was telling. "The Knarr don't want the war to restart any more than we do."

"I hope not, but we don't know how many are loyal to Vander and won't question him. Go on, you don't have much time."

"And you?" Amber demanded. "I'm not leaving you. You're mad if you think I am."

"They need one of us to convince Dad and Marra, and I'm faster than you."

"But you can't go alone. What if they catch up with you?"

"I'll go with her," said Brede.

"You're their leader. You need to go with them."

He shook his head. "I'm the leader of our hunting party. Storegga is more of a community leader than I am." The mermaid with the patchy tail looked at him, a flicker of surprise in her eyes. Brede shrugged. "Anyway, I'm already wearing the amulet."

"Fine," Jet said. "We don't have time." Brede jerked his chin at her in acknowledgement, and various members of his party handed him weapons and armour that he strapped to himself like a patchwork. Jet looked between them, her gaze landing on Amber. "Go, stick together, use your strengths."

Amber groaned. "I don't like this. I'll get back to you as soon as I can."

"Just keep them all safe."

Amber nodded, and then she was gone. Jet took a calming breath, gills flaring. "Right, your hearing's ridiculously good, isn't it?"

He nodded matter-of-factly.

"Great. We'll go back the way we came, slowly. You listen out for Vander and his group."

"And then attract their attention," he said, nodding. "Tempt them away from the others."

"I hope so. I'm hoping Vander's group isn't big enough to separate effectively. He only came with two."

Brede glanced at her. "I'd be surprised if he hadn't organised a larger group to follow."

"Yeah." She sighed. She jerked her chin at the blades he was strapping to his tail. "At least I know you're a good warrior."

He gave her a crooked smile. "And you will not have to worry about your mage this time." His attention snapped into the deepening blue toward nothing Jet could detect. "They're coming."

"Close enough to hear me if I yell?"

"Not yet," he said. "But they're fast."

Jet snorted, her heart thumping with adrenaline coursing through her in the mounting anticipation. "I'm faster than any Knarr."

Brede smirked. "Big words from a little *Farm* Deeper."

"Race you?"

"Oh, you've no chance against me. I'm no longer Knarr, am I? I'm a Hvaler."

She tilted her head. "Hvaler, huh? That's what you're going for? What does that mean?"

He actually looked a little shy. "Whale. But it's what all Knarr call hunters like us, the ones who can hunt like orca."

"Huh," she said. "I assumed it was because you hunt whales."

He looked horrified. "No, why would we eat whales?" When she shrugged, he rolled his eyes. "They're sacred to us."

"Oh. Yeah, okay." She nodded. "It's a good clan name. Hvaler."

"Jet," he said. "We should go. Now."

"Shit, right." She cupped her hands round her mouth and yelled, "This way, Amber! We've got to get to Whitby beach." Then the two of them turned and sprinted. "Too obvious?" she panted.

"No time for subtlety," he shouted back, and they bent their heads, flattened their hands to their sides, and beat their tails onward.

CHAPTER TWENTY-TWO

This is becoming a habit, Tessa thought as she lowered herself to the concrete slope outside Jet's beach hut. At least she didn't have wine this time.

Her eyes still ached, and her skin was still hot from her confrontation with Hannah. Part of her was furious with herself. She should have had more self-control.

The other part knew that was Hannah's voice in her mind. She'd felt out of control for so long, and trying to learn the kind of composure that Hannah wanted from her had done nothing but make her feel like a failure.

She couldn't blame Hannah for all of it, though. She'd taken a few comments, a few events, and had run with them, building walls around all the broken parts of herself and pretending that covering them up was the same as healing. It wasn't.

She shuffled back and leaned against Jet's door. She wondered if that was as close as she'd ever get to her again, and she regretted trying to build those walls back around her heart when Jet had had to leave. It had felt important, then, a survival strategy, and now it felt like a waste of time.

"Tessa?" called a voice, and she squinted into the sunset.

"Sophie?"

Sophie ran up to her, coat flapping around her calves. "I thought that was you. How are you? Oh, mind the dog…down, Pickle! Sorry about that."

Tessa couldn't have cared less about sandy paws on her lap and scooped the puppy up as best she could, cooing over him. "He's gorgeous, oh my gosh, I'm going to steal you away."

Sophie laughed and pulled herself up the railings to sit next to Tessa. "You're welcome to him at four in the morning when he starts whining to go out for a wee. Is your family okay?"

Tessa nodded. "Yeah. Nephew's now safely back home." She snorted. "I assume he is."

Sophie was quiet for a minute, eyes searching Tessa's face. "Are *you* okay? And before you automatically say you're fine… are you *really* okay?"

Tessa gave a hopeless laugh and stared out to sea as the puppy crawled onto her lap and squirmed around, seeming to turn himself into knots to get every inch of fur stroked. "I don't think I'm fine," she admitted.

Sophie nodded and followed her gaze. The seagulls and the surf of the incoming tide filled the silence between them, and Tessa was left space to just breathe. There was nothing Sophie could have done to make it better, but having her there, a witness, was a comfort Tessa could never have predicted.

"I had an argument with my sister," Tessa said at last. Sophie tilted her head and hummed her interest. "She's always wanted me to be perfect. I thought it was because she wanted me to be better, be safe, you know? But it's because she's scared."

"And you? Are you scared?"

"Yeah." Tessa laughed. "But I want to be who I am too, you know?"

"Mmm, I do."

"I called my old therapist this afternoon. I'm starting back up with her. She always used to talk about embracing what you feel and who you are, but I couldn't…I just couldn't back then."

"Hey, that's great, though. Good for you." Sophie thumped her on the back, and Tessa shot her a grin.

"I wish I'd figured it out before Jet left. Wish I'd told her."

Sophie nudged her with her shoulder as if the comfort lying in the air between them was no longer enough, and she wanted to push it into Tessa's skin. "Can you text her?"

Tessa shook her head. "Kinda hard to get in touch with her. She's a bit…off-grid."

"I hope she comes back for you, mate. She should. You're a total catch."

Tessa laughed and rolled her eyes, then startled as the words landed. "Wait, did Elliot tell you? That I'm gay?"

"Uh, no, sorry, was it a secret? Shit, I assumed. I mean, the way you talk about her, I thought she was your girlfriend."

Tessa couldn't help but smile as she nudged Sophie back. "No, it's fine. I guess I'm not as good at hiding it as I thought." Her smile disappeared as she thought of sitting next to Jet, talking about politics and life under the sea and Tessa's work. She'd thought so much of it was a story. She'd wasted so much of the little time they'd had.

"Aw, Tessa, you really fell hard, huh?" Sophie said softly. "Can I give you a hug?"

Tessa didn't answer, just leaned slightly toward Sophie in case she wanted not to notice, wanted to retract the offer. But Sophie wrapped her arms around her and pulled her down, tucking Tessa's face into her bird-like shoulders.

Her phone rang, and she leaned back with a little smile at Sophie. She groaned as she looked at the name popping up on her phone. "It's my sister. The other one."

"You want to ignore it?"

The phone rang out and was silent a moment before immediately starting up again. Tessa rolled her eyes. "No, I'll deal with her."

Sophie winked and picked Pickle up. "I'll leave you to your family drama, then. You've got this, Tess. See you tomorrow."

"Thanks, Sophie," she said. She took a deep breath and pressed *answer*. "Hello?"

"Tessa. Where the fuck are you?"

"Jesus." Tessa winced and pulled the phone away from her ear. "You don't need to deafen me."

"Tessa, what the fuck's been going on? I go to lectures for a few days, like you guys are always telling me to, I might add, and suddenly, you grow a pair of balls and tell Hannah she's a homophobic bitch. I am *hurt* and *offended.* Why didn't you invite me to the show?"

"Oh my God," Tessa groaned. "You're such a bloody drama queen."

"Where *are* you? I've been to your house, and you're not there. Don't tell me you got a life in the last few weeks."

She shook her head but gave in. "I'm down by the beach huts near Dan and Ellie's rental."

"Do not dare to move."

She hung up, and Tessa tucked her phone in her pocket, leaning her head back to watch the seagulls wheel overhead. Her eyes were hot, and her head ached, but there was a strange peace in her heart that she could hardly recognise. It was the same thing she felt when she pulled a big job off, like she'd done something *right* that she could stand by.

Joanie took just over a minute to get to her, pulling her beaten-up little sports car into the parking space on the top of the cliff, loud EDM pumping until she cut the engine. "Tessa," she yelled, leaning over the railing. She waved wildly when she saw her. "Stay there."

"I'm not a dog," Tessa yelled back half-heartedly.

Joanie ran almost the whole way down the slope, doubling back at each hairpin turn until she reached the beach huts and stood with her hands on her hips. "Explain yourself, young lady."

"Well," said Tessa. "One day about thirty-two years ago, Mum and Dad decided to have a little brother or sister for their first-born daughter, so they—"

"Shut up, you know what I mean."

"I'm sorry, do you want me to shut up or tell you stuff? You're giving me very mixed messages here."

Joanie groaned loudly and tugged on her hair. "You're the worst." She flopped next to Tessa and glared at her. "If my tights ladder on this rough-ass concrete, I'm stealing some of yours."

"Good luck with that. I don't wear tights."

Joanie groaned again. "I can't believe you yelled at our big sister and called her homophobic and racist—"

"I didn't call her racist. I told her that *Ben* thought she was being racist."

"What? She didn't say that. Why did Ben think she was being racist?"

"Because Hannah can't get her head out of her arse."

Joanie waited a beat. "No, I'm gonna need more details than 'Hannah being Hannah.' What did she actually do? Because I just had to deal with her in actual tears on the phone, sobbing about how she's the worst person in the world, and we all hate her, so spill."

Tessa sighed and relented. "You know Ben told her about Jet, that she's a mermaid?"

Joanie laughed. "Oh yeah, that girl who was trying to teach him how to use a spear? He wouldn't shut up about her on the drive back. I'm not surprised he told Hannah."

Tessa grimaced. "Well, Hannah thought that 'mermaid' was some sort of slang for lesbian or girlfriend or something. She told him he had to stay away from people like her."

Joanie shrieked with laughter. It went on quite a lot longer than Tessa thought was acceptable, and she made a show of checking her watch. "That's all it took?" she said at last, wiping tears out of her eyes. "Mermaids? Really? That's the hill you're willing to die on?"

"It's not the mermaid thing. It's the principle of it. She's so determined to force everything around her into this perfect 'normal' mold that she's alienating her own son. If she doesn't get her shit together, she's going to lose him. Did she tell you he ran away? No, I didn't think so. Also, did she tell you that Dad *and* Mum both knew I was gay for years? They just never bloody talked about it. That's what's wrong with this family. Nobody ever fucking *talks* about anything, and it's tearing us apart."

All the humour left Joanie's face, and she nodded. "Yeah, well, I've been trying to tell you guys this for about ten years, but why would you listen to your baby sister? What do I know?"

"You—"

She snorted and turned away, looking out over the sea. Tessa thought about how much easier it was to say hard things while looking out over the waves, throwing the words into the ocean where their sharp edges could be worn down before the sea threw them back. "Why do you think I don't go and see Hannah much? Or even Ben? I can't stand the way she tries to pretend everything's perfect all the time. It's not. It hasn't been since... since Mum and Gabe died." She hunched her shoulders. "I barely remember them, Tessa. What did Gabe sound like? Because in my head, he only sounds like you."

"And Dad—"

She made a sharp noise in her throat and wiped her nose, and Tessa realised with horror that she might be crying. "Dad can't even remember my name. What's fucking normal about that? We keep pretending that it's okay. Why do we do that?"

Tessa reached for her hand, rubbing her thumb over Joanie's smooth skin. "Because he doesn't always forget. The times he remembers make up for it." She shrugged. "I'm not pretending it's okay, it's not. It sucks, and it hurts, but I'm also not going to pretend he's already dead."

"Like them," she said, turning red eyes on Tessa, daring her to pretend.

"Like them." Tessa nodded. "It's not okay. It never has been."

"We need so much fucking therapy," said Joanie, and a tear escaped and ran down her cheek.

Now it was Tessa's turn to reach out and pull someone close, rocking them as they cried. She stroked Joanie's hair and kissed the top of her head and cried a little more for the brother who'd never gotten to grow up, the mum who would've been much better at this than her.

As Joanie's tears abated, she shifted to lean against Tessa, and together, they stared out over the water, still and rose-glowing in the last rays of the sun. "We're a mess," said Joanie, wiping her face on her sleeve.

"Yup."

There was a weird disturbance on the surface of the water, a bubbling and roiling. She'd only ever seen something like it on Attenborough programmes, when the dolphins attacked a bait ball, or whales made bubble rings. "What's that?" Joanie said, sitting up and frowning, squinting into the last of the light.

Tessa was climbing to her feet when the water seemed to explode, two figures barreling out as if made from cork and landing hard on the beach. "Jesus," Joanie cried, shrinking back, but Tessa was already running toward them.

"Brede," yelled Jet because it was her, it was *Jet*, and Tessa wasn't sure whether to laugh or cry or panic because something was wrong. "Get up, we've got to keep moving."

The other figure, bare-legged with a long black and silver tunic twisted around him, pushed himself up on his arms and tried to get his feet under him. "I can't…I've never…"

Jet ran over to him, her legs just as bare, and was that Tessa's hoodie? Only stretched somehow into some sort of weird dress? "Jet," she screamed.

"Tessa?"

Tessa threw herself at Jet, clutching her close, not caring about the soaking-wet clothes and hair. "Tessa," Jet gasped, panting hard like she'd been running for miles. "You can't be here, you've got to go, run." She gripped Tessa's jacket, though, fingers tangling in the material bunched around Tessa's waist.

Tessa squeezed her tight one more time, then turned to the man, still stumbling and struggling to his feet. She lifted him and slung one arm over her shoulder. "Come on, I'll get you back to my place."

"No, you can't. It's too dangerous."

"You've got other mer chasing you, haven't you?"

Jet nodded, glancing back. If Tessa squinted, she thought she could see dark shapes beneath the surface, humps of water lifting, not quite waves. Her skin prickled at the fear in Jet's eyes.

"Let's go. Quick."

"Tessa, what's going on?" Joanie said, hovering a few feet away, staring at Brede.

"We've got to get these guys somewhere safe," she said, glancing back at the shapes now disappearing in the dusk. Jet tucked herself under Brede's other arm, and together, they dragged him onward.

"I'm fine," he said. "I just need time."

"Well, that's something we don't have," Jet said. "Flatten those feet, that's right, roll them. Heel, toe, heel, toe."

He stared down at his feet, bare toes digging too deep into the sand as he seemed to try to grip with them, the muscles not quite coordinated. Tessa glanced up at Jet, who looked pale and drawn, dark circles under her eyes, the exhaustion not just from her most recent flight.

There was a massive thrashing, churning noise, and Tessa startled round to look at the waterline. "Traitor," screamed a creature in the surf, and Tessa clutched at Jet, everything in her demanding she get out of there. "Traitor and murderer, come here and face me, you cowards!"

"What the fuck?" cried Joanie, staggering backward. "That's…"

"Vander," said Jet. "Come on, we have to go."

"I'll find you," Vander screamed, his tail thrashing, turning the water to foam. He started pulling himself forward on his elbows, and other mer appeared beside him, tugging him back into the water. "Jet, you bitch, I'll find you, I'll take you back to your bastard parents, and you'll watch me kill them. I'll kill them all."

Jet tensed, but Brede gripped her upper arm. "Come on, Jet."

"What if he goes to them first?"

"He won't," Brede said. "He'll bring out his witch first."

Jet's head snapped around. "His what now?"

"I'll tell you, but we must *go*."

"Come on, back to mine," Tessa muttered. "Joanie, you too."

Joanie shook her head, her eyes still wide and terrified, but Jet nodded. "You must. We should stick together. I don't know whether Vander saw you or not, but you'll be safer with us."

"Or far away from you and whatever the fuck *that* was." She gestured back to the water, which was now calm again.

"We have weapons," Brede said, a vicious looking knife appearing in his hand. "Vander will too. Do you have enough to protect yourself alone?"

"Jesus, where were you hiding that?" Tessa muttered, leaning back.

"I wasn't hiding it." He sheathed the knife back somewhere in the sleeve of his tunic. "But the point stands."

"Okay," Joanie said, nodding, her voice slightly high with hysteria. "Fine. Hot guy with a knife. Great." She pointed at Jet. "Wait. You're an actual fucking mermaid? That was *real*?"

Tessa squeezed her eyes shut. "Could we please get back to my place?" It was going to be a long night. "Joanie, give us a lift, would you?"

She looked at Tessa like she'd just kicked a puppy. "Are you fucking kidding me? On the leather?" She gestured at them. "They're dripping seawater, and probably blood judging by knifey-boy here."

"Joanie!"

"Anyway, it's a two-seater, you know that."

She pinched the bridge of her nose. "Fine, yeah, I forgot."

"You forgot about my baby? How could you?"

"It's an old fucking Mazda, not a Lambo, for God's sake." She shook her head and pulled Brede's arm back over her shoulder. "Sorry," she said to him. "It's not far."

Chapter Twenty-three

Jet focused on helping Brede to find his feet, pulling him out of the way of traffic and ignoring the stares they got from passing humans. She was painfully aware of Tessa walking on Brede's other side, bickering with Joanie. Were they okay? Was that hug on the beach an indication of how Tessa felt, or would it go back to the coldness from before she'd left?

Tessa opened her door and ushered them inside. "Jet, you and Brede need a shower. Will you show him how to use it? Get warmed up. You're welcome to borrow clothes."

She glanced at the hoodie which now stretched down to Jet's knees, modified by the amulet's magic. "I'm sorry, I ruined it," Jet said.

She shook her head. "No, I gave it to you." She ran her fingers through her hair and looked away. "To remember me. I'm glad you're wearing it." Jet smiled as Tessa blushed. "Go on, get warm," Tessa said, a little huffy, and Jet gave her hand a squeeze as she ushered Brede past and up the stairs.

"How's your arm?" she asked him as she adjusted the water temperature.

Brede tugged his tunic down to expose a vicious red welt where one of Vander's men had caught him with a projectile. "It's fine," he lied, the lines of tension around his eyes tightening as he brushed it.

"They poisoned that thing, didn't they?"

He nodded. "Weever fish spines, I think." He pointed at a row of puncture wounds over his bicep. "Lucky I'm left-handed. Don't worry, I'll still be able to fight."

"Good. I'll see if Tessa knows a human remedy. Shower's ready now. Remember to take your clothes off before you get in. Salt left behind on your skin after the water's evaporated itches like crazy, so humans wash their clothes in fresh water."

"Like from estuaries?" he said, eyebrows raised. "Weird."

"Smells great, though. Oh, and put this stuff in your hair, then wash it all out. Trust me."

He looked skeptical but took the bottle of conditioner from her as she left the bathroom and went to nose through Tessa's drawers again. She'd have to find something for Brede to wear too, maybe an oversized T-shirt of some sort. For a mer, he was surprisingly lithe, which now that she thought about it, probably made him more streamlined for hunting. But in his human form he towered over Tessa, and his bulk would never squeeze into one of those tight, stretchy shirts of hers. His blond hair was as long and tangled as Jet's too, and she hoped, selfishly, that Joanie would brush his for him, not Tessa.

She straightened up as footsteps sounded on the stairs. Tessa froze as she got to her bedroom door, and they gazed at each other, the moment fragile. "I'm sorry," Tessa blurted. "I was scared. I didn't want you to go."

"I didn't want to go either," Jet whispered. "I *wanted* to want to go. I wanted it to be easy, but it wasn't."

Tessa crossed the short distance between them and held Jet's cheeks, kissing her gently, deeply. "I know you can't stay forever. I'm not asking that."

"But I want to come back." Jet gripped Tessa's arms, pressing their foreheads together. "Wherever I go, know I don't want to, okay? I may have to—"

"Of course, I know, your people. They're important to you, I know."

Jet nodded and swallowed. "I killed someone," she whispered, and Tessa gasped. "Back before I came here. I didn't know, but he died of an infection after…"

"Oh God, Jet," she said. "Oh God, that's awful."

Jet hid her face in Tessa's shoulder. "I'm scared, Tessa."

Tessa wrapped her arms around Jet again, not seeming to care that Jet was still wearing the soaked hoodie. "What can I do?"

Jet clung to her a moment longer. The maelstrom of fear and relief swirled in her head so violently, she didn't want to emerge from the safety of Tessa's arms, but that safety wouldn't last. Vander would be coming for them.

"Brede's been injured," she said at last. "The Knarr have projectiles lined with weever fish or man-o'-war poison. Do you humans have anything to treat them?"

"I'll search it. What about that man, the mer in the water, he said…"

Jet nodded, swallowing. "Vander. I don't know what his next move is going to be, but Brede's clan has gone to warn mine. They should be protected."

Tessa nodded, fishing out her phone and typing. She looked up and must have caught some of Jet's uncertainty because she cupped Jet's cheek. "Hey. We'll get through this, okay?"

Jet closed her eyes and nodded, pressing into Tessa's warm hand. She had to believe it.

The bathroom door opened behind them, and the floorboards creaked as Brede stepped out. Jet turned to see him standing awkwardly on the landing, the towel held against himself like a sheet. "Human bodies are very strange," he said to Jet, his voice shell-shocked.

She laughed. "I know, aren't they just? It always takes me a few days to get used to how big breasts can be."

Brede looked down at himself, then back up, his eyes still wide. "Breasts are not the main concern for me."

Tessa made a strange snorting noise and shoved an armful of clothes at him, muttering something unintelligible. Her face was flame-red as she scuttled down the stairs. Jet shrugged and let herself into the shower.

CHAPTER TWENTY-FOUR

The first thing Tessa saw when she entered the living room was Joanie curled up under Mum's old afghan, staring at the blank wall. "You bitch," Joanie said. "Mermaids are real, and you didn't tell me."

Tessa laughed softly. "Sorry, I didn't feel like convincing you I'm not insane."

Joanie let out a long breath. "We're not, though, are we? It's not some shared hallucination?"

"There's a merman upstairs who looks traumatised by his own penis. I don't think I'm imaginative enough to hallucinate that."

Joanie made a weird noise between a laugh and a hiccup. "Oh God, they don't have…well, I guess not, I mean, where would they keep them?"

Tessa blinked at her. "Where would they *keep* their penises?"

They looked at each other a moment longer, then burst into hysterical laughter, trying to keep their voices down and nearly crying with the effort. "It wouldn't be very hydrodynamic, would it?" gasped Joanie.

"I haven't thought about it that much," Tessa said. "I don't think about penises much at all."

"Fucking hell, would you stop saying penis?"

One of the mer upstairs dropped something, the bang making them both jump. Joanie wiped her eyes and tugged the afghan over her head. "Do I really have to stay here? Am I really in that much danger? I want to go home, Tess."

"I don't know. I'm sorry."

The stairs creaked, and Tessa leaned back to see Brede coming down, his attention fixed on the slope in front of him. "Shit, weever fish," she said, tapping her head.

"What about them?"

"Brede got hit with some sort of weever fish dart. Jet asked me to research treatment."

"Hot water and painkillers," said Joanie promptly. "Remember Ahmed, that boyfriend I had in year eleven? He stood on one. They hurt like hell but won't kill you or anything."

She nodded and gestured to Brede to follow her into the kitchen. Joanie trailed them, the afghan still over her shoulders. She sat next to Brede at the table. "So," she said, narrowing her eyes at him. "You're a merman, are you?"

"I suppose," he said. "Though not currently."

"Yeah, speaking of that. What happens to your tail when you shapeshift or whatever? Does it split in half? Does it hurt?"

"Joanie, leave the guy alone," Tessa said, rolling her eyes.

"Hey, I'm just trying to break the ice."

"I don't mind," said Brede.

She shrugged and left them to it, boiling water for tea and for Brede's treatment. Jet came downstairs with a towel over her shoulders and a comb. "Would you mind? Later?"

Something felt like it was glowing in Tessa's chest. There was an enemy to battle, a wounded merman in her kitchen, and a sister who was going to have even more questions the longer she had to think about it, but right now, Tessa had never been happier. She leaned forward and kissed Jet softly on the cheek. "Of course. For now, though, Joanie says weever fish treatment is just hot water and painkillers." She handed some ibuprofen and a glass of water to Brede.

"Here," said Joanie, pulling the bowl of hot water toward her. "I'll do this. Which arm?"

Brede unzipped his hoodie and pulled the material halfway down his right arm. A shallow cut ran across his bicep, still bleeding sluggishly. Around it, big yellow blisters were forming, and his skin was swollen, hot to the touch, and tight. Joanie and Tessa hissed in sympathy. "Okay," Joanie said. "You have to have the water as hot as you can stand. It won't cure it, but it'll help with the pain."

"We have to talk about Vander," Jet said, sitting forward and catching Brede's attention while Joanie started pouring water from a cloth onto the wound.

The skin around Brede's eyes tightened from the pain, but he nodded at Jet. "I'm sure he'll go back for his witch," he said.

"You mentioned that before. I thought the Knarr didn't have magic users."

"They're rarer than in Farn Deeps but not unheard of. That's why he keeps her close."

Jet frowned. "What, they live with him?"

"Just one now," he said. "Since the war. He…he keeps her locked away."

Jet's eyebrows shot to her hairline. "He what? Why?"

Brede looked to the side. "I don't know. He never said himself, but there are always rumours. Always different. How she was dangerous and he kept her locked up for her own good. That she went mad with grief after her fellow witches were all killed in the war. Some say she's his sister, and, well…after he lost his brother…"

"This witch," Joanie said. "You think Vander's going to, what, get her to put a curse on Jet?"

"Amber says curses aren't a thing," explained Jet, her voice muffled by her hands pressed against her face. "I don't understand it all, but it's more immediate, more right in front of you. She could hit me with a spell if she could see me but not from a distance."

"She could find us, though," said Brede. "There are definitely seeking spells. He had her find a child who went missing, caught in a current. I don't know how they work, but that's why I said you should stay with us." He gestured at Joanie, who made a face but otherwise kept working on his arm. "I don't know if they would be able to seek you out too."

"Why would they bother?"

"To keep the secret, apart from anything," said Tessa. "Humans aren't supposed to know about you, are we?"

Jet shook her head. "It's not like we make an effort. We don't tell humans much and let them draw their own conclusions about us."

"And Knarr don't go on land much," added Brede. "That's very much a Farn Deeps thing."

"What are we going to do?" Jet asked him, leaning forward. "We can't wait here for them to catch us."

"I have a car," Tessa said. "We can all leave tonight."

"And then what?" Joanie said. "Tess, I've got uni tomorrow. I've got a life."

"And I don't?" Tessa snapped. "I know you think my work is boring, but it matters, I love it, and I'm damn good at it. But this could be life or death."

Joanie stood, slapping the table. "And it could all be for nothing. What then? Do we keep on running forever? I'm not doing this, Tess."

"Look, nobody's running anywhere," said Jet, standing and holding her hands out.

"Indeed," said Brede, frowning at the table. "If we run, we lose what advantage we do have. If we stand and fight, we set the battlefield."

"And what do we *humans* do?" said Joanie, throwing her hands up. "I don't know about you guys, but my sword-fighting skills are a bit rusty."

"Swords," Jet said to Brede. "We could try out cutting blades. Those work much better on land than underwater, much less resistance."

"I suppose it would be," he said. "Any weapon that you swing would be better. Tessa, do you have any swords?"

The two mer looked at her with identical gleams in their eyes. Tessa held up her hands. "That's not something most humans have lying around the place. Best I can do is a kitchen knife."

Joanie groaned, long and harsh. "This is ridiculous." She dumped the cloth back into the bowl of water and shoved her chair close to the table.

"Where are you going?" asked Brede. "You must stay here, it's safer."

"I don't know," she snapped. "The living room? Spare room? Anywhere away from this little war council you've got set up here. Is that close enough for you, your majesty?"

"I'm not royalty," he muttered, cowed. Joanie flicked her hair and stomped out.

"I'll ring for pizza," Tessa yelled after her, then turned back to Jet. "But seriously, do you think it's going to come to this kind of a fight? Is there any chance we can talk him down?"

Jet looked to Brede, who twisted his lips. "I hope so, but it depends on what happens between now and then. Whether the people around him want to fight or not, whether they think they'll get something out of it personally."

"That's depressingly like humanity," said Tessa.

"For now, we have to assume that he'll fight. We can try to convince him otherwise when we get the chance," said Jet. "Let's plan accordingly. What weapons do we have?"

A vicious blade appeared in Brede's hand as if from nowhere. "I have this. My caudal blades seem to have changed shape thanks to Amber's amulet. They now strap to my legs."

"Jesus," said Tessa, leaning back. "You've got two of those?"

He nodded and waggled the blade in Jet's direction. "I hope they'll turn back when we get to the water."

"They'll be fine. What did you make those out of? I've never tried caudal blades. How do you find they work for you?"

"Can we discuss weaponry after we've made a plan?" Tessa said.

"Weapons are *part* of the plan," Jet said with a whine.

"Not mermaid, sorry, *mer* weapons. We need land weapons." She pulled a pad of notepaper and a pen from a stack on the table. "What does Vander usually fight with? What will limit him on land?"

"Gravity," said Brede. "He fights fast, like Jet, and he uses all his space. Not being able to swim above his opponent will disadvantage him."

Tessa hummed. "Gravity works against all of you, though."

"What weapon does he favour?" asked Jet. She glanced over at Tessa. "This is relevant this time, promise."

"Daggers," said Brede, flipping his blade so it lay back against his forearm.

"Then he's used to close combat," Jet explained to Tessa. "And means my spear will have a longer range."

"How about going out to the moors," suggested Tessa. "Miles of open space. We'll be able to see him coming."

"Don't forget there are others," Brede pointed out. "Any benefits to you could be benefits to them too, and we don't know if they'll have other poisoned blades." He gestured at his arm, still swollen and red around the wound.

Jet glanced at Tessa, and for a moment, Tessa could see the fear behind her drive and bravado. The seriousness of the situation was sinking deeper; this could either mean running away to God knew where or fighting and possible injury. Either way, nothing would be the same again. She was going to lose something, some part of her old life, and never get it back.

She reached over and linked hands with Jet, tangling their fingers together. "We'll get through this," she said firmly. "Whatever needs to be done."

Jet held her gaze and nodded, then took a deep breath. "Let's go to the moors, then, shall we? We don't know how long they'll be."

Tessa nodded, grabbing her phone. "I'll order pizza, and we can pick it up on the way. Joanie?" she called. "Do you want a meat feast?"

There was no answer, and she sighed. "Jet, could you check upstairs, please? She's probably fallen asleep."

Tessa checked the sitting room, then looked up the stairs as Jet came back down. She knew it was all going to shit the moment she saw Jet's face, and her mind backdated her fear. She'd known when she'd called out and Joanie hadn't answered. She'd known when Joanie had stomped off. She'd known when Tessa and Brede had burst from the sea. She'd known when that train had rolled off the tracks and turned her life upside down, kept turning it and turning it.

"We've got to find her," she said, and she could barely breathe. Joanie was going to get caught by a murderous merman, and Tessa was going to lose another sibling. It would be her fault Joanie got dragged into this. "I have to find her, I have to."

Jet grabbed her biceps and gave her a little shake. "Hey, listen, she'll be fine. We'll find her, you hear? She can't have gone far."

"Vander will find her, won't he? Oh God, he'll hurt her…"

Jet glanced over Tessa's shoulder. "He wouldn't be looking for her straightaway, would he, Brede?" He didn't answer, so Jet pulled Tessa close, wrapped her strong arms around her, and Tessa burrowed into her comfort, her breath coming too quickly.

Then the door exploded behind her, the shockwave shoving them against the stairs and Brede into the living room. Tessa sat up, dazed, her ears ringing, and pain speckled across her arms and back where shards of wood had bitten into her skin.

"Stay back, Vander." Somehow, Jet was already standing, a short spear in hand.

"You thought you would play the same trick, did you? Splitting up may have served you the last time, but I'm not an idiot."

The terrifying mer from the beach was no less intimidating in his human form, as muscular and heavy as all mer seemed to be. His black hair was twisted up and out of the way, exposing a network of scars across his face and vicious, hate-filled eyes.

People were screaming somewhere. Brede crouched on the floor in the living room, out of sight of Vander. She thought about old Enid next door, how scared she'd be. *Not relevant, not important right now.* She tried to clear her head, to *think*, but every signal was telling her to run, find a way out, and there was none she could see, none that would keep Jet and Brede safe too.

"These people are innocent. Your fight is with me," said Jet, stepping sideways to shield Tessa.

"There is no innocence or guilt in war," said Vander, snorting, and Tessa had a wild urge to tell him about the Geneva convention. "Because this *is* a war, and you've spilled first blood."

"Fine," said Jet, through gritted teeth. "You want a fight that bad, you've got it. Bring it on, old man."

Chapter Twenty-five

Jet clutched her spear as she logged everything around her, the slippery debris, the small group of Knarr behind Vander, Tessa's location. This was far from their plan to wait for Vander out on the moors, but perhaps they still had an advantage. The stairs gave her possible high ground, and the corridor was narrow enough that the other Knarr had no hope of joining the fight without pushing past Vander.

Vander laughed and drew his daggers, wasting no time darting forward, slashing at Jet. She brought up her spear, and he stabbed underneath her guard. She twisted her spear at the last moment, knocking the second blade back with a grunt. She heard Tessa gasp and scramble back up the stairs out of the way. Vander jumped back, and Jet narrowed her eyes, dropped her stance a little lower, thinking of the surfboard and hoping that Brede was right, that balance would be something Vander had never had to think of.

He darted forward, and Jet spun her spear, catching the haft of it against one of his wrists and then kicking the other. Vander snarled, rolling with the strike, ducking in close. Jet only just dodged, the blade slicing into the shirt over her belly. She turned the spear, jabbed the haft toward his face. He blocked, but it gave her enough time to shift away from the stairs so she could back up. Not too soon. She didn't want the other Knarr getting to Tessa. Just enough that he'd follow her, strike again, and *there*.

Jet held her spear in both hands and trapped his left hand against the wall as he rushed at her. Every unprotected inch of her body tingled as she exposed her side to him, and the moment stretched into eternity.

Until Brede slammed into Vander, trapping his other arm, his own blade at Vander's throat.

"Hold," Jet shouted at the Knarr. "Stay where you are, or we kill him."

"Traitor," Vander snarled at Brede. "Treacherous bastard *freak*."

Jet let out a long, shaky breath and met Brede's eyes. "Thanks."

"How did you know I would be here?"

She laughed, high and hysterical, and twisted Vander's hand behind his back, pushing him in front of her. "I didn't. Just hoped you'd be up for an opening, being a hunter."

"Crazy farmer."

Tessa leaned over the edge of the stairs dangling a belt. "Will this work to tie his hands?"

Jet smiled up at her, pride swelling in her chest at the human who'd never seen battle and winced at blades but kept her head when she needed to. "Yeah, that's great," she said as Brede took it and wrapped Vander's wrists behind his back, pulling it tight. She turned him, pushed him in front of her, and walked to the doorway, Brede by her side with his knife at Vander's throat.

Glass and debris crunched underfoot as they approached the ring of the Knarr. Jet glanced around, noting the difference between these mer and the ones she'd fought in the buffer zone. These were stoic, trained, and mostly her parents' age. Mer who'd fought in the war. Soldiers. None of them were shifting and muttering the way Gul, Brede, and Haj had, and she swallowed the lump in her throat.

"We have your leader," she yelled, hoping her fear didn't show in her voice. "Who has the authority to treat on his behalf?"

"I do," said a pale-eyed mer in the middle of the semicircle. "I'm General Saeby."

"Give her nothing," Vander spat.

Saeby didn't even look at Vander, which gave Jet dangerous amounts of hope. "Do you want a war, General?" Jet asked. What kind of mer clan had generals, anyway?

Saeby's eyes flickered around the rest of the mer. "We will do what must be done."

A fair answer and one that seemed to piss Vander off, judging by the way he was straining at the belt around his wrists. "Where are the rest of you?" she asked. "The witch and the others?"

Saeby conferred with the mer next to him. "They are on their way."

"They have your little pet human," Vander said, and though she'd expected it, Jet still felt a swoop of fear in her stomach. She glanced over at Tessa, whose face was pale.

"Have them release her when they get here. I want your assurance that the Knarr will not pursue a war with Farn Deeps *or* with the newly formed Hvaler clan. Only then will I release Vander."

"Don't you fucking dare, Saeby," yelled Vander. "Kill them all, kill the bastards."

Saeby glanced at Vander for the first time and seemed to stand even straighter, staring at nothing. "Agreed," he said, and Vander howled wordlessly, thrashing in Jet's grip.

"You'll swear to that when your witch arrives," Jet pointed out.

Saeby nodded and turned to the other mer, who held a device like a human mobile to his ear, talking quickly into it. "They will meet us at the north beach," he said.

Jet patted Vander's shoulder. "Great. After you, Chief."

"Fuck off."

Brede growled under his breath and shoved Vander, and the four of them stepped forward, the Knarr forming an honour guard of sorts, a horseshoe of twitchy soldiers leading the way. Jet's eyes flickered from one to another. "No projectiles today?"

"They're inaccurate on land," Saeby said shortly.

"Lucky us."

Vander twisted in her grip, and she pressed the blade against his throat just hard enough to break the skin. "You are exactly like your father," he muttered.

"Yeah, well, at least we move on from the past," said Jet.

Vander barked a laugh so hard, the blade pressed in, drawing a bead of blood. "From the girl who attacked a group of Knarr three decades after the war?"

"Shut up."

Tessa moved closer. "Where is everyone?" she said softly. "My door was blown off. Someone will have called the police, but there's no one."

"It's the spell," said Brede. He tapped his ear. "Can't you hear it?"

Jet frowned. "Spells make a noise?"

He shrugged. "Your witch nearly deafened us when she cast that spell on you. The amulets seem to be silent, though, unless I hold them up to my ear."

"Huh," Jet said.

"Freak," said Vander.

"You see, this is why the Knarr have lost all their best hunters," said Brede, shoving Vander forward.

CHAPTER TWENTY-SIX

The eerie quiet continued throughout the walk down to the beach. The streets were empty, and their shuffling footsteps echoed. Tessa kept herself tucked behind Brede and Jet as much as she could. She would only get in the way in a fight. She didn't want to put the others in more danger by getting attacked herself.

The moonlight shone on the sea, casting a silver glow over the north beach as they made a strange procession down to the waterline. A second band of mer stood waiting for them, and Tessa almost cried out as she saw Joanie held between two mer.

"Tessa!"

"Joanie, it's okay," Tessa yelled, trying not to let her fear show.

"I'm sorry. I should've listened." Joanie's voice was muffled, like she'd been crying.

A silver-haired woman—a mermaid, Tessa assumed—snapped her fingers, and Joanie's voice disappeared. Brede winced like a sharp sound was hurting his ears, and Tessa had to dig her fingernails into her palms to ground herself, remind herself not to leap forward for Joanie. She was stamping her feet now, her mouth moving soundlessly as she swore at the witch.

"She'll be fine," said Jet. "I promise, we'll get her back."

The Knarr who'd led them to the beach gathered around Joanie's guards, facing off against them. General Saeby gestured to the witch, and they stepped forward. "Jet of Farn Deeps, do you speak for your clan?"

"I do," Jet said, straightening from where she had been using Vander as a shield. Tessa assumed there was some sort of tradition in the words, maybe something that promised safety. "Brede of the Hvaler speaks for his own."

"Hvaler?" The witch's eyebrows raised.

Brede glanced at Jet, a flash of fear in his eyes. "I…yes. We can't live in Fiskebank. The noise is making us ill."

Saeby sighed. "The noise. The noise that nobody else can hear?"

"I can hear it," said the witch. The Knarr general did a double take that would have been amusing in any other situation. "Oh, as if any of you would ever ask *me*. Or release me from my bonds so I could do something about it."

Saeby blinked and shook his head. "We will discuss this later. What are your terms, Jet?"

"We will release Vander safely once you release Joanie," said Jet, and Tessa's chest ached in relief.

"Of course," said Saeby, turning to Joanie's guards.

"I'm not finished," said Jet quickly. "We need your assurance that you will no longer seek war with any of us, not Farn Deeps, the Hvaler, or the humans. Not for this."

"Don't you fucking dare." Vander twisted in Jet's grip, spitting his words. Both she and Brede had to cling on to him.

"This is an uneven trade," said Saeby, barely glancing at Vander. "It should be one person for another."

"He's your chief," Jet said. "Surely, he's worth more to you than the average person."

Saeby glanced at a couple of others, and Tessa strained every sense, needing advance warning for every move.

"Perhaps he is not," Saeby said at last, and a murmur went through the Knarr, a change in their stance or demeanour, nothing Tessa could pinpoint, but something absolute all the same.

"Wait," Brede said, his jaw dropping. "He's not what?"

"Our chief."

There was a beat of shocked silence, then Vander roared with rage, thrashing in his bonds until Brede and Jet had to knock him to his knees, clinging to him. "Witch! This is your doing. Traitors," Vander howled. "Traitors, every one of you."

Saeby swallowed and seemed to stand more stiffly to attention. "The Knarr are not averse to peace, though," he continued and paused for Vander's rage to swell up again.

The witch rolled her eyes and snapped her fingers, and Vander was left squirming and thrashing in silence. "Ah, Vander. You should've kept my shackles on." She tutted and twisted her hands, making sparks and bright patterns roll between her fingers.

Saeby glanced wide-eyed at the witch, then swallowed and straightened up again. "We want the treaties rewritten," he said to Jet. "We cannot move forward as a people when the humans take up so much of our space and apparently drive off our best hunters. We need cooperation between our two…three clans."

"I may be able to help with that," said Tessa before she could overthink it. Saeby looked at her, his eyebrows shooting up. Tessa glanced to Jet, who shrugged and made a *go on* gesture as well as she could with her hands full of a still-raging Vander.

Tessa took a step forward and bowed awkwardly. "Please excuse my intrusion. I'm Tessa Bordeaux, I work for a company that tries to encourage the use of sustainable technology. I've seen organisations that try to prevent oil companies from using things like sonar air guns. Maybe I could offer my services to you or put you in contact with some researchers?"

Saeby turned to talk with his advisors, then back. "We will take it into consideration, thank you. I don't think the Knarr are ready to officially treat with humans yet, but perhaps some way can be found." He turned to Jet, now standing as Vander seemed to have collapsed in despair. "This all started with your actions, though."

Jet glanced up at Tessa and swallowed hard. "I know," she said. "By my actions, one young merman is dead, and I don't want to avoid punishment. But I can't let my people suffer because of it. Take me prisoner, even…even kill me, but I need your word that you won't go to war over this. Please. Let me be the end."

Tessa's heart dropped as Jet spoke, her body feeling bloodless and numb at the thought of Jet being taken away, even killed. Her fingers twitched to reach out, to grab Jet's shoulder, but she couldn't distract her. She knew how important her family was, all her people. Jet glanced up, her dark eyes terrified and sorry, and Tessa held her gaze even though it hurt.

"Your death would not bring him back," said Saeby at last, and Tessa found herself crying, the despair and relief coming so close together that her body couldn't take it. Jet tore her gaze away from Tessa's and up to Saeby.

"Have her teach," said the witch. "Vander never wanted the war mentioned, but he wanted weapons in every hand and witches like me locked away safely until we could be pointed like a bomb in the right direction." She spat on the ground. "If you truly don't want war, you'll tell every child of our clans why. Gul was little more than a child himself."

Jet nodded vigorously. "I swear," she said. "I…I know it doesn't help, but I've regretted it every moment since I found out. I'm sorry."

Saeby nodded but didn't meet her gaze. Tessa wondered, wiping her face, if he'd known the boy that Jet had killed. The witch held out her hands and closed her eyes. "Come forward, clan representatives," she said, and her words seemed to have weight to them.

Brede pushed to his feet beside Jet, rubbing his ears and grumbling. The two of them stepped forward to meet Saeby. "The Knarr pledge to return the human Joanie Bordeaux to her family and return to Fiskebank with no further desire for war."

"Farn Deeps pledges to return Vander to his clan, and I, Jet, pledge to teach the dangers of battle to young people in every clan, every year, in memory of Gul."

"The Hvaler pledge to release Vander to his clan and..." Brede hesitated and glanced at Jet, then spoke in a rush. "And offer to trade the spoils of our hunts with both clans."

Jet smiled. "Farn Deeps pledges to renegotiate the terms of the treaty with both clans and offers to set up trades."

"The Knarr also pledge to renegotiate the treaty with both Farn Deeps and Hvaler and to trade."

The three of them looked around at each other, then nodded to the witch. She began to chant, and a ball of light formed between her two hands, glowing and brightening until it outshone the moon, and Tessa had to turn her face away. When she looked back, the three of them had a band of light around their wrists.

Jet rubbed her wrist under the bright light, then looked up to the witch, speaking quickly. "If you want, my cousin's a mage. She can help you get away."

The witch snorted in amusement. "Sweet child. I didn't bide my time for this long just to lose my power as a refugee. Trust me, my shackles aren't going back on." She turned to Saeby, who swallowed and looked away. She smirked and stretched her arms. "Now, no offence to the humans present, but legs are exhausting. Let's be done with this." She flicked her wrist. "Take your person, and we'll take ours."

"Joanie." Tessa took a tentative step forward, and Joanie burst into tears, running toward her.

Joanie was at arm's length when Tessa felt the air punched out of her lungs as strong arms wrapped around her middle. She was lifted off the ground, and for a moment, she was twelve again, suspended breathless in midair as the train carriage and bodies and broken glass spun around her. Joanie's scream broke through the years and the panic, and Tessa was back on the beach, strong arms around her waist and dragging her toward the water. Jet was running after her, and Tessa's gaze met hers.

Her own terror was reflected in Jet's eyes.

The cold water hit Tessa's back and went over her head, and she clapped a hand over her nose and mouth on instinct. She turned, her eyes burning from the salt, and saw Vander's sharp teeth bared, his nose and ears sinking back into his face. Then he kicked his tail, and the water forced its way between her fingers, up her nose.

She could feel her heart beating, her lungs screaming, adrenaline and panic flooding her veins, demanding that she breathe, *breathe*. It didn't *matter* that there was no air, every muscle wailed for her to *breathe*.

She was going to die here, dragged into the black depths of the North Sea.

Lights were sparking in her eyes. Her ears exploded with pain from the pressure, but it hardly registered against the all-encompassing panic of airlessness. She was going to die.

Something pale glinted against the dark press of the sea. A weak beam of moonlight on a spearhead, maybe? Or a hallucination? Either way, determination cut through the panic whirling through Tessa's mind, and she shifted her face to bite down hard on the arm wrapped around her shoulders.

She heard the wild scream and tasted the sharp tang of blood. The relentless rush of water stopped, and the arm shifted, so she bit somewhere else, again and again. Blows hammered into her ribs, and she felt the last bubbles of air pushed from her body, and with the last ounce of strength she had, she *bit*. She clamped her jaw around Vander's arm, malice and spite and the last rational thought, *I hope Jet doesn't feel bad for killing this one*.

Then, everything was perfectly calm. Water found its way into the vacuum of her lungs and she hung, drifting in space, awareness narrowing down to a point, to blood and water and a flash of a dark tail like a magpie's wing.

CHAPTER TWENTY-SEVEN

Jet had never been so afraid. She swam after Vander and Tessa, and every moment she knew in her bones that she couldn't possibly catch him on time. Tessa couldn't hold her breath that long, not that deep.

She thought she'd caught Tessa's gaze at one point when she was gaining on them, but she would be too late. She thought she could see the hope and despair in Tessa's eyes, but humans couldn't see much in salt water. It had to have been her projecting…

And then Tessa, brilliant, foolish Tessa, had bitten him. Human teeth were not made for that kind of thing, but she'd bitten his arm and held on, digging those blunt things into his flesh until he had to stop, until he'd *beaten* her, and she'd *still* kept biting.

Jet had screamed her throat raw. When Tessa had gone limp, she'd become nothing more than a being of rage. She'd thrown her spear, something utterly stupid that she never would have tried if she'd had any rational thought left in her. Spears didn't work underwater the way they did in air.

Vander should have been able to knock it aside.

Instead, it rammed into his throat. Jet flung herself on the shaft and drove it forward, deep and down, blood spilling into the water like a fountain, stinking of grief and everything terrible. She didn't have time to care and hate herself because Tessa was limp, eyes shut and mouth slack, and Jet had to take her to the surface, had to hope. Had to try.

CHAPTER TWENTY-EIGHT

Tessa woke to a steady beeping sound and a heavy weight on her arm. When she moved, a hand pressed against her forehead. "Hey," said Amber. "Can you hear me?"

She opened her eyes, wincing at the light and the scratch of her own eyelids. She was in hospital with Joanie lying asleep on her arm and Jet's cousin Amber fussing over her like a nurse.

Amber tapped her ears and pointed to Tessa. "Yeah," said Tessa, or tried to. She ended up coughing, and with it came an echo of that panic, the loss of air.

"Tessa? Hey, it's okay, you're fine, just breathe." Tessa felt Joanie's arms around her and leaned toward them, clutching at her clothes, taking gulping, bubbling breaths. Joanie clung back, holding her tight and safe. "Amber, can you—"

"Yeah, yeah, I'm doing it." Amber pressed warm hands onto Tessa's back, and with the next cough, she sputtered water out of her nose and mouth.

"Oh God," she groaned. "Oh, I'm sorry, that's disgusting."

Joanie laughed and wiped both of them off with coarse blue tissue. "I'm just glad you're awake."

"How long's it been?"

"Two days, you bitch. I'm still salty about it. If the Knarr witch lady hadn't been there on the beach, you'd have drowned." Joanie punched her arm.

"Ow," whined Tessa.

"Amber here's been doing this crazy mermaid magic shit, sucking water out of your nose while the nurses aren't looking. It's wild."

Amber winked at her and stood. "Speaking of, the nurse asked me to tell her when you woke up." She pulled the curtain aside and slipped out.

Joanie leaned her elbows on the bed. "I think Amber's got a crush on the nurse," she said. "Or else, she's got an intellectual crush on human tech and medicine. I can't work it out. Either way, she's been taking notes. She's almost as much of a nerd as you are."

Tessa was losing the battle against her exhaustion, her eyelids drooping already. "Where's Jet?" she asked. Her eyes snapped open. "She's okay, right?"

"Yeah, she's fine," said Joanie. "She's been here as much as she can, but apparently, the treaties need rewriting or whatever. Between you and me, I think she's scared you'll hate her."

"What? Why?"

Joanie shrugged. "You tell me. People like you and her, you're all the same, always blaming yourself for everything. Dummies."

Tessa bit her lip. "Can you tell her I don't?"

"You can tell her yourself," said Jet from the door, and Tessa's smile felt like it could split her face.

"Oh my God," Joanie said, rolling her eyes. "That's it, I'm out. You two can be gross together."

Tessa reached out, and Jet walked over to take Joanie's space, gripping her hand tightly. She bent down to kiss Tessa on her temple, on her lips, on her cheek. "I was so worried," she whispered. "I'm sorry I put you in danger."

Tessa grabbed her around the waist and held her close as best she could with the canula in her arm. "Shut up," she said. "You saved me. You're here. That's all that matters."

Jet crawled onto the hospital bed and curled around her, head resting on Tessa's shoulder. "I'm sorry," she whispered again.

"You have nothing to be sorry for."

"I have so much to be sorry for. Not just to you. I killed someone else. I would do it again for you, but…"

Tessa kissed her and stroked her hair. There was nothing to say. She couldn't know what Jet was going through, but she didn't need to. All she needed was to be there for her.

❖

Tessa looked up at the front of her building, assessing the repairs. "They've done a good job, haven't they, love?" Enid called, leaning out of a window in her own house.

"It looks good as new," she agreed. "Did they fix yours up okay?"

"Aye, and it was a good excuse to visit my friend Heidi down in Scarborough. Did you stay with your sister, then?"

"No, with Sophie from work." She tried to imagine crashing on Joanie's dorm room or even speaking to Hannah and had to suppress a shudder.

"Oh, the little lass you've told me about? That's nice of her. Now, I've got a pineapple upside down cake in the oven. Will you pop over for a cuppa and a slice to celebrate later?"

She grinned up at her. "Wouldn't miss it, thanks, Enid."

Enid nodded, looking pleased with herself, and retreated inside, leaving Tessa to peace and solitude and the slightly daunting prospect of seeing her house for the first time after the fight.

She felt like broken glass should be crunching under her feet as she entered, that everything that had happened was too big to have been cleared away in such a short time. It had been less than a week, and Tessa had a front door again, a clean corridor, and a working pair of lungs.

She trailed her fingers along the wall as she walked up the steps, remembering the fear, the screams, the dust. Vander snarling in the hallway. Vander dragging her down. She had to stop a moment and take a deep breath of air. *You're safe. He's dead.*

She unpacked her little bag, rolling her eyes at the mess Joanie had made of her drawers when she'd come to collect clothes for her. It wasn't that she was ungrateful, but did Joanie really have to take all the clothes out and dump them on her bed? She could've just grabbed the first shirts and trousers she'd found.

When there was a knock at the door, she assumed it would be Joanie. Maybe Enid or a postie. If she was really lucky, it would be Jet, back from Farn Deeps early.

It was Hannah.

"Hi," said Hannah. She sounded quiet. Had Hannah ever said *hi* to Tessa in her life? She'd always come in mid-rant.

"Hi."

Hannah looked away and tucked her hair behind her ears, bit her lips, tapped her fingers. Distantly, Tessa wondered how long she could keep her hanging there, waiting. Instead, she huffed. "I'm going to make some tea, do you want some?"

She turned, leaving the door open, and Hannah mumbled something, shutting the door behind them. Tessa focused on the actions of tea-making, then stopped, her hand hovering over the sugar bowl. "I've no idea how you take your tea." She turned and leaned against the sink, crossing her arms over her chest.

Hannah stood in a mirroring pose at the kitchen doorway. "I…suppose I don't know how you take yours."

The silence was only broken by the rising bubble of the kettle. Tessa watched Hannah's uncharacteristic awkwardness and tried to stop herself from analysing her. Things needed to change in their family. Tessa didn't want to try to predict her sister. If she wanted something, she was going to have to say so.

"I spoke to Ben," she said at last.

"That's good," said Tessa, nodding.

Hannah cleared her throat. She still wasn't looking at Tessa. "And I spoke to Jeremy. Joanie too, even."

"Wow." She wasn't trying to be sarcastic. It seemed to be happening by itself.

"What do you want from me?" Hannah snapped, looking at Tessa at last.

"Nothing," said Tessa, unable to stop a dry laugh. "Is this how the talking went with the others, though?"

Hannah growled wordlessly and pinched the bridge of her nose. "Why do you always have to be so difficult?"

Why do you have to be so difficult?

I'm not trying to be difficult.

I just want to make you happy.

Tessa threw her hands up and pushed all the words on the tip of her tongue away. They all felt too hurt and vulnerable for right now. "What are you hoping to get out of this? Why are you here?" *If I'm so fucking difficult.*

"I want to hold this family together. I can't bear to see it torn apart like this."

"And what would that look like to you? The family together?"

"What do you mean?"

Tessa sat down, elbows on the table, and jerked her head to the chair opposite until Hannah took the hint. "What's important about family to you?"

Hannah rolled her eyes, sitting right at the edge of her seat, her knees pointing to the door as if she was ready to race out of there. "God, you look like you're about to take notes, like this is some sort of business meeting."

"That's not a bad idea, actually." She pulled the notepad and pen toward her from the usual pile in the middle of the table. The top page had scribbled bullet points about weapons and moorland, and Tessa hesitated before turning to a fresh one, laying it out clean and fresh.

"You can't be serious."

"Why not? I'm good at stuff like this."

"We are a family, not a problem to be solved by committee."

"I think we've got plenty of problems to solve," Tessa countered. "Healthy communication being the main one. What have you got to lose by trying it my way?"

"Fine." She clenched her jaw and sat straight, glaring at Tessa over her handbag. "Well, then. How do we do this Tessa's way?"

"As I said before. What do you want to keep the same about this family?"

"Everything. I just want things to be like they were."

"Well, I don't."

Hannah blinked. "What? Why?"

"The way things were fucking sucked. Not just for me but for all of us. You can't honestly say you were happy running around frantically trying to whip us all into perfection, can you? Because I'm damned if I'm going back into the closet for you."

"I never wanted you in the closet. I didn't know that Dad knew. I really thought he'd be upset."

"So it wouldn't bother you if I brought my girlfriend to dinner? Sat next to her on the sofa, held hands with her in front of Dad?"

Hannah scoffed. "You hardly need to flaunt it in front of everyone."

Tessa closed her eyes. "Flaunt what? The fact that I have a girlfriend? The fact that I'm gay?"

"It's nothing to do with that. You're putting words in my mouth."

"So it was flaunting it when you held Jeremy's hand all through Christmas drinks at the home last year?"

"Well, that's..."

"You need to think really fucking carefully about this, Han, because you're either telling me that it's okay if I'm gay as long as I hide it, or you're telling me that you don't want to see me getting affection from someone I love. Or both."

Hannah's eyes were starting to well up, her shoulders rounding and hunching. "I'm not saying that," she said, her voice small. "I'm not homophobic."

"Are you not homophobic?" Tessa asked, holding her sister's gaze firmly. "Or do you not want to be homophobic? Because if you're going to keep on saying these homophobic things, insisting that they're *not* homophobic, then we have a problem. But if you *want* to change…"

"I just want everyone to be safe and happy," she whispered. "That's all I've ever wanted."

Tessa swallowed her own hope, the urge to take it as an apology, the easy road. "I want that too. But I wasn't happy, I was ashamed of being me. I need you to try, okay?"

Hannah nodded. Tessa reached across the table, squeezed her hand, and allowed herself a little sliver of hope for the future.

EPILOGUE

Six months later

Tessa opened the door of Jet's beach hut to look out at the sea skeptically. "Are you sure I won't freeze my arse off?"

Jet chuckled. "Come on, it's well into spring, and the amulet will change your physiology. Even a skinny thing like you will cope with it."

Goose bumps pricked along Tessa's skin and she shuddered. "Fine. But I'm wearing that wetsuit top too."

"Good plan," said Jet. She came up behind Tessa and began to tie the amulet around her neck, then kissed her on the shoulder. "Are you ready?"

She took a deep breath and nodded. "Oh sure, just magically change species and go meet my girlfriend's parents, totally ready."

Jet laughed and linked their hands, tugging her down to the beach. She was wearing the same strangely distorted hoodie that Tessa had given her that first time, her own amulet a dull gold against the hollow of her throat.

The water was freezing and the April sky overcast and threatening rain. Tessa tried not to show how cold she was, her legs already tingling. She held tighter to Jet's hand, and together, they walked into the waves.

"You ready?" Jet yelled as they reached chest depth.

Tessa nodded. She wasn't. As they jumped to duck completely under, she had a panicked memory of Vander's arm around her waist, dragging her down.

The moment the water closed over her head a warm glow flowed through her. She fought the urge to scream as her legs seemed to be pulled together against her will, fusing and reshaping in ways she could barely conceive of, her feet flattening and stretching, her muscles spreading.

"Open your eyes," said Jet, her voice impossibly clear and close. Tessa did so, expecting the dark, low visibility that she usually got when she fell off her surfboard.

Instead, the world was a bright, clear blue, her eyes picking up every weak beam of light filtering down from above. Jet, noseless, earless Jet, gently tugged her hand away from her face. "You can breathe now. Trust me?"

Tessa took a cautious breath, and then gasped in shock at the feeling of water flooding her throat but not her lungs. She touched her neck, wincing as a finger slipped into a sensitive gill slit. The gills fluttered.

Jet gave her a tentative smile. "Okay?"

Her hair was a vast halo around her head, each strand thicker and sensitive, like the feathers on a fan worm. Tessa put her hand up to her own hair and nearly went cross-eyed with the jumble of sensations. Her hair was still short in comparison to Jet's, but she could *feel* sounds and currents and Jet's small movements as water shifted through the strands.

"Do you want to go back?" Jet asked. "Or carry on? Either is fine, really."

She looked different. Tessa had thought Vander looked a little like Voldemort without a nose, his face smooth and streamlined, but on Jet, it didn't seem to make much difference. Her dark eyes were bigger, her black hair a miracle, and her tail…once she saw it, Tessa couldn't take her eyes off it.

Jet had once described her tail as black and iridescent, and it really was. Streaks of purple, green, and blue shifted with the light coming down from the surface, the translucent caudal fin fluttering as she made small movements to keep herself steady.

"You're as beautiful here as you are on land," Tessa said.

Jet's eyes widened, and then she grinned, her cheeks pinking. "Wow, you're such a flirt."

"Only with you." Tessa touched her cheek, noting every difference to the usual feel of her, the change to her skin and her bone structure. "How does it feel to kiss underwater?" she asked, and the whole ocean seemed to be much smaller all of a sudden, just the two of them and nothing else.

"You looking for a demonstration?" asked Jet.

Tessa nodded and leaned forward to kiss her, pull her closer, and press their bodies together. Jet's tail wrapped around hers as far as it could go, and Tessa lost herself in the feel of Jet's lips and tongue, her sharp teeth, and the whole ocean making itself part of their kiss.

Farn Deeps was going to have to wait. Tessa wasn't going to rush this for anything.

About the Author

Lyn Hemphill is Kenyan born and bred but now lives in Oxfordshire with her partner and two children, who like to help her come up with some more outlandish plot points. She writes every spare moment she can find, in between teaching science online and developing screenplays with her writing partner, Aloïs Castel.

Books Available from Bold Strokes Books

Almost Perfect by Tagan Shepard. A shared love of queer TV brings Olivia and Riley together, but can they keep their real-life love as picture perfect as their on-screen counterparts? (978-1-63679-322-1)

Corpus Calvin by David Swatling. Cloverkist Inn may be haunted, but a ghost materializes from Jason Dekker's past and Calvin's canine instinct kicks in to protect a young boy from mortal danger. (978-1-62639-428-5)

Craving Cassie by Skye Rowan. Siobhan Carney and Cassie Townsend share an instant attraction, but are they brave enough to give up everything they have ever known to be together? (978-1-63679-062-6)

Drifting by Lyn Hemphill. When Tess jumps into the ocean after Jet, she thinks she's saving her life. Of course, she can't possibly know Jet is actually a mermaid desperate to fix her mistake before she causes her clan's demise. (978-1-63679-242-2)

Enigma by Suzie Clarke. Polly has taken an oath to protect and serve her country, but when the spy she's tasked with hunting becomes the love of her life, will she be the one to betray her country? (978-1-63555-999-6)

Finding Fault by Annie McDonald. Can environmental activist Dr. Evie O'Halloran and government investigator Merritt Shepherd set aside their conflicting ideas about saving the planet and risk their hearts enough to save their love? (978-1-63679-257-6)

Hot Keys by R.E. Ward. In 1920s New York City, Betty May Dewitt and her best friend, Jack Norval, are determined to make their Tin Pan Alley dreams come true and discover they will have to fight—not only for their hearts and dreams, but for their lives. (978-1-63679-259-0)

Securing Ava by Anne Shade. Private investigator Paige Richards takes a case to locate and bring back runaway heiress Ava Prescott. But ignoring her attraction may prove impossible when their hearts and lives are at stake. (978-1-63679-297-2)

The Amaranthine Law by Gun Brooke. Tristan Kelly is being hunted for who she is and her incomprehensible past, and despite her overwhelming feelings for Olivia Bryce, she has to reject her to keep her safe. (978-1-63679-235-4)

The Forever Factor by Melissa Brayden. When Bethany and Reid confront their past, they give new meaning to letting go, forgiveness, and a future worth fighting for. (978-1-63679-357-3)

The Frenemy Zone by Yolanda Wallace. Ollie Smith-Nakamura thinks relocating from San Francisco to her dad's rural hometown is the worst idea in the world, but after she meets her new classmate Ariel Hall, she might have a change of heart. (978-1-63679-249-1)

A Cutting Deceit by Cathy Dunnell. Undercover cop Athena takes a job at Valeria's hair salon to gather evidence to prove her husband's connections to organized crime. What starts as a tentative friendship quickly turns into a dangerous affair. (978-1-63679-208-8)

As Seen on TV! by CF Frizzell. Despite their objections, TV hosts Ronnie Sharp, a laid-back chef; and paranormal investigator Peyton Stanford, have to work together. The public is watching. But joining forces is risky, contemptuous, unnerving, provocative—and ridiculously perfect. (978-1-63679-272-9)

Blood Memory by Sandra Barret. Can vampire Jade Murphy protect her friend from a human stalker and keep her dates with the gorgeous Beth Jenssen without revealing her secrets? (978-1-63679-307-8)

Foolproof by Leigh Hays. For Martine Roberts and Elliot Tillman, friends with benefits isn't a foolproof way to hide from the truth at the heart of an affair. (978-1-63679-184-5)

Glass and Stone by Renee Roman. Jordan must accept that she can't control everything that happens in life, and that includes her wayward heart. (978-1-63679-162-3)

Hard Pressed by Aurora Rey. When rivals Mira Lavigne and Dylan Miller are tapped to co-chair Finger Lakes Cider Week, competition gives way to compromise. But will their sexual chemistry lead to love? (978-1-63679-210-1)

The Laws of Magic by M. Ullrich. Nothing is ever what it seems, especially not in the small town of Bender, Massachusetts, where a witch lives to save lives and avoid love. (978-1-63679-222-4)

The Lonely Hearts Rescue by Morgan Lee Miller, Nell Stark, Missouri Vaun. In this novella collection, a hurricane hits the Gulf Coast, and the animals at the Lonely Hearts Rescue Shelter need love, and so do the humans who adopt them. (978-1-63679-231-6)

The Mage and the Monster by Barbara Ann Wright. Two powerful mages, one committed to magic and one controlled by it, strive to free each other and be together while the countries they serve descend into war. (978-1-63679-190-6)

Truly Wanted by J.J. Hale. Sam must decide if she's willing to risk losing her found family to find her happily ever after. (978-1-63679-333-7)

A Good Chance by Ali Vali. Harry, Desi, and Desi's sister Rachel are so close to getting everything they've ever wanted, but Desi's ex-husband is coming back to get his revenge and rip apart their chance at happiness. (978-1-63679-023-7)

A Perfect Fifth by Jaycie Morrison. Streetwise pianist Zara Keller and Lady Jillian Stansfield couldn't be more different; yet their connection brings a new awareness of who they are and what they truly want in their lives—including each other. (978-1-63679-132-6)

Catching Feelings by Ana Hartnett Reichardt. Andrea Foster expected to catch a lot of pitches from the Alder Lion's star pitcher, Maya, but she didn't expect to catch feelings. (978-1-63679-227-9)

Defiant Hearts by Lee Lynch. In these stories, you'll find your lovers, friends, and lesbians you wish you knew—maybe even yourself. (978-1-63679-237-8)

Love and Duty by Catherine Young. All Princess Roseli wants is to marry her three lovers, but with war looming, she must instead marry Princess Lucia to establish a military alliance between their planets. (978-1-63679-256-9)

Murder at Union Station by David S. Pederson. Private Detective Mason Adler struggles to determine who killed a woman found in a trunk without getting himself killed in the process. (978-1-63679-269-9)

Serendipity by Kris Bryant. Serendipity brings jingle writer Annie Foster and celebrity pop star Bristol Baines together, and their undeniable attraction keeps them close, but will their different paths drive them apart? (978-1-63679-224-8)

The Haunted Heart by Jane Kolven. A ghost, a ring, and a quest to find a missing psychic—it's a spell for love. (978-1-63679-245-3)

The Rules of Forever by Nan Campbell. After reconnecting at their high school reunion, Cara and Lauren agree to embark on a textbook definition friends-with-benefits relationship, but trying to keep it uncomplicated is harder than it seems. (978-1-63679-248-4)

Vision of Virtue by Brey Willows. When virtue and desire come together, be prepared for sparks in this next installment of the Memory's Muses series. (978-1-63679-118-0)

Cherry on Top by Georgia Beers. A chance meeting leaves Cherry and Ellis longing for a different life, but when Ellis's search for truth crashes into Cherry's insta-filter world, do they have any hope at all of a happily ever after? (978-1-63679-158-6)

Love and Other Rare Birds by Angie Williams. Ornithologist Dr. Jamie Martin and park ranger Rowan Fleming are searching the Alaskan wilderness for a bird thought to be extinct and they're about to discover opposites really do attract. (978-1-63679-108-1)

Parallel Paradise by Mayapee Chowdhury. When their love affair is put to the test by the homophobia of their family, community, and culture, Bindi and Rimli will need to fight for a chance at love. (978-1-63679-204-0)

Perfectly Matched by Toni Logan. A beautiful Cupid named Hannah, a runaway arrow, and just seventy-two hours to fix a mishap that could be the best mistake she has ever made. (978-1-63679-120-3)

Royal Exposé by Jenny Frame. When they're grouped together for a class assignment, Poppy's enthusiasm for life and love may just save Casey's soul, but will she ever forgive Casey for using her to expose royal secrets? (978-1-63679-165-4)

Slow Burn by Missouri Vaun. A wounded wildland firefighter from California and a struggling artist find solace and love in a small southern town. (978-1-63679-098-5)

The Artist by Sheri Lewis Wohl. Detective Casey Wilson and reclusive artist Tula Crane are drawn together in a web of passion, intrigue, and art that might just hold the key to stopping a killer. (978-1-63679-150-0)

The Inconvenient Heiress by Jane Walsh. An unlikely heiress and a spinster evade the Marriage Mart only to discover true love together. (978-1-63679-173-9)

A Champion for Tinker Creek by D.C. Robeline. Lyle James has rescued his dad's auto repair business, but when city hall condemns his neighborhood, Lyle learns only trusting will save his life and help him find love. (978-1-63679-213-2)

Closed-Door Policy by Erin Zak. Going back to college is never easy, but Caroline Stevens is prepared to work hard and change her life for the better. What she's not prepared for is Dr. Atlanta Morris, her gorgeous new professor. (978-1-63679-181-4)

Homeworld by Gun Brooke. Headed by Captain Holly Crowe, the spaceship Velocity's crew journeys towards their alien ancestors' homeworld, and what they find is completely unexpected—and they're not safe. (978-1-63679-177-7)

Outland by Kristin Keppler & Allisa Bahney. Danielle Clark and Katelyn Turner can't seem to stay away from one another even as the war for the wastelands tests their loyalty to each other and to their people. (978-1-63679-154-8)

Secret Sanctuary by Nance Sparks. US Deputy Marshal Alex Trenton specializes in protecting those awaiting trial, but when danger threatens the woman she's falling for, Alex is in for the fight of her life. (978-1-63679-148-7)